Wanda E. Brunstetter

SHILOH kidz
An Imprint of Barbour Publishing, Inc.

Print ISBN 978-1-62836-389-0

eBook Editions:
Adobe Digital Edition (.epub) 978-1-63058-967-7
Kindle and MobiPocket Edition (.prc) 978-1-63058-968-4

All German Dutch words are from the Revised Pennsylvania Dutch Dictionary found in Lancaster County, Pennsylvania.

Cover illustration by Colleen Madden/MB Artists

Published by Shiloh Kidz, an imprint of Barbour Publishing, Inc., P.O. Box 719, Uhrichsville, Ohio 44683, www.shilohkidz.com

Our mission is to publish and distribute inspirational products offering exceptional value and biblical encouragement to the masses.

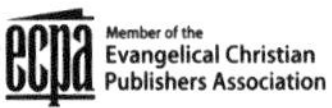

Printed in the United States of America.
04813 1014 DP

To my Amish friends,
who know what true humility is about.

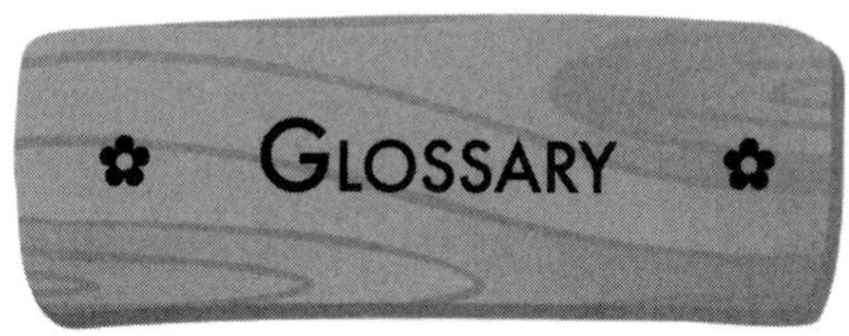

absatz–stop
ach–oh
appeditlich–delicious
bauchweh–stomachache
blumme–flowers
brieder–brothers
bruder–brother
daadihaus–grandparents' house
daed–dad
danki–thanks
dumm–dumb
eefeldich–silly
felse–rocks
fenschdere–windows
grank–sick
grossmudder–grandmother
guder mariye–good morning
hochmut–pride
hund–dog
hungerich–hungry

Is gut.—It's good.
jah—yes
katze—cats
kichlin—cookies
kinner—children
kumme—come
mamm—mom
naerfich—nervous
schlang—snake
schmaert—smart
schocklaad—chocolate
schuhbendel—shoelace
umgerennt—upset
wasser—water
wendich—windy
Wie geht's?—How are you?

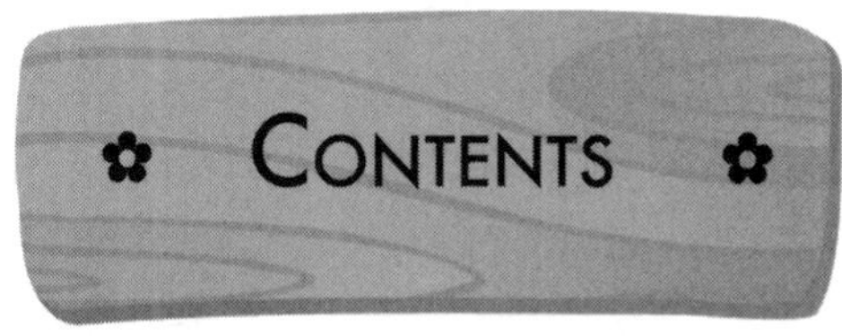

Contents

1. Mattie's Mistake . . . 9
2. Broken Glass . . . 18
3. Found with the Trash . . . 27
4. Test Results . . . 36
5. No Fun Jumping Rope . . . 46
6. Mattie Hides Out . . . 56
7. Last Day of School . . . 61
8. The Flu Bug . . . 69
9. Change of Plans . . . 78
10. Trouble with Twinkles . . . 88
11. Good News . . . 98
12. Stella's Visit . . . 108
13. A Bat to Catch . . . 118
14. Broken Latch . . . 129
15. Blueberry Pie . . . 137
16. Birthday Surprise . . . 148

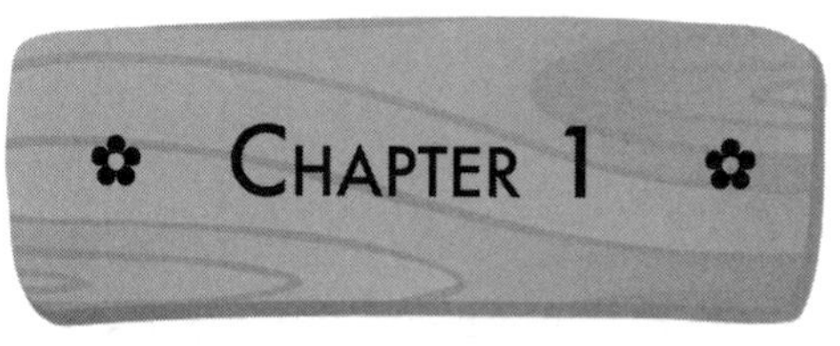

Mattie's Mistake

"Hey, Mattie, come see what I found," Mark called to his twin sister from across the yard. The sky had finally cleared after a couple of days of rain, and even though the grass was still wet, it felt good to finally be outside again. He was glad this was Saturday and he and Mattie had time to play.

"Can it wait?" Mattie hollered. "I'm playing fetch with Twinkles right now."

Mark wrinkled his nose as he watched the little brown-and-white terrier zip back and forth across the yard in pursuit of a small red ball. He couldn't believe Mattie would rather play fetch with her dog than see what he'd found a few feet from their barn. After all, it wasn't every day that he discovered not one, but two unusual stones. "Mattie, *kumme*," Mark said. "I want you to see these *felse* I found."

"Maybe later I'll come and look at the rocks," she said, bending down to pick up the ball again.

Mark figured Mattie would probably forget all about

his rocks, since she wasn't a rock collector. *Where have these pretty stones been all this time, and why haven't I noticed them before?* he wondered. *I'll bet all the rain this past week made them rise to the surface.*

Mark squatted down for a closer look. One of the rocks was black with silver flecks, and the other was gray and shaped like a duck. At least Mark thought it looked like one. Part of the rock resembled a beak, and another section reminded Mark of a duck's tail feathers stretched way back.

Mark had been looking for special rocks since he was six years old, when he'd discovered a large flat stone that looked like a pancake. Now, Mark was almost ten, and he'd collected lots of rocks for the last four years. He kept them in cardboard boxes underneath his bed and would often take them out and count every single one. Then he'd write down the amount in a notebook, along with a description of any new ones he'd found. Sometimes when Mark found a special rock, he would draw a picture of it and put that in the notebook, too. Rock hunting was a fun hobby, and Mark had been surprised to learn that Mattie's friend Stella collected rocks, too. Stella showed Mark her collection once, and although she had some nice ones, Mark thought his rocks were the best. Too bad he couldn't get Mattie interested in looking for unusual stones.

It was odd how different rocks could be, but then he thought about how people were different, too, because everyone was unique. Like a snowflake, no two were alike. Other than the fact that Mark was a boy and Mattie was a girl, most folks couldn't tell by just looking at them that they were nothing alike. They had the same red hair, blue eyes, and a few freckles. Their personalities and the things they enjoyed doing were not the same, however. Mark was full of adventure and liked to use big words. He collected rocks, went fishing whenever he could, and loved his two cats. Mattie enjoyed drawing pictures and planting flowers, and was good at playing baseball. She preferred dogs and didn't care much for cats. His twin sister also liked to make up silly songs that rhymed.

A gentle breeze came up, and Mark's thoughts turned to the weather again. Springtime was in full swing in Walnut Creek, Ohio. The warmer temperatures, not too hot and not too cold, made it hard for Mark to be inside when he wanted to play. When it rained, he either had to stay in his room or find something to do out in the barn. He was glad he could be outside today.

Mark glanced at the clean sheets hanging on the clothesline, drying in the wind. It would sure smell good when Mom put those sheets on his bed tonight, with the fresh scent of outside air. This kind of weather made Mark feel energetic—like there was a spring in his step.

A bird chirped from a tree in the yard, and Mark smiled. Except for the ones that wintered in Ohio, most of the other birds had returned a few weeks ago from their winter homes south of Ohio. Spring was nesting time in nearby trees and in the bird boxes Grandpa Miller had made. One of the boxes hung on the post connected to the fence that ran along their backyard, and soon after it had been put up, a pair of pretty bluebirds had claimed it.

Earlier this spring, everyone in Mark and Mattie's family had watched anxiously each day as the bluebirds flew back and forth, bringing nesting material to the box until it was completed. After that, they saw the male more often, sitting on top of the birdhouse or in one of the trees in their yard. The female bird flew out sometimes, but never for long, since she was sitting on eggs. One day Mark had waited until she flew out. Then he climbed a ladder and took a peek. Sure enough, four powder-blue eggs lay in the nest.

"Sure wouldn't be throwing that ball in close proximity of our bluebird box, Mattie," Mark called.

Her forehead wrinkled. "*Proximity*? What's that?" she asked, moving closer to Mark. "I've never heard that word before."

"It means 'near,' or 'close,'" he explained.

"Why didn't you just say that then?"

Mark snickered. "Because I like to use big words."

"*Jah*, I know." Mattie grunted. "I think you do that just to show off."

"No, I don't." Mark motioned to the bird box. "If you throw the ball over that way, it could make the birds feel *naerfich*, and they might abandon the nest."

"Don't worry, I'll be careful," Mattie said.

Mark scooped up the two rocks he'd found and held them out to Mattie. "I want you to see what I found. Aren't these great?"

"They're okay, I guess," Mattie said, barely glancing at the rocks. She picked up the ball Twinkles had dropped at her feet and gave it a toss. The ball landed near the fence along the driveway.

"How was that for a good throw?" Mattie asked, smiling widely. "Bet you can't pitch a ball that far."

"You're right, I probably can't, but have you ever thought about teaching Twinkles something else besides retrieving a ball?"

"Like what?" Mattie wanted to know. "She already knows how to speak, sit up and beg, and walk on her hind feet."

"How about jumping through a hoop?"

Mattie shook her head. "I've tried that already with my Hula-Hoop, but it's a hard trick, and she won't do it."

Mark lifted his chin and grinned at Mattie. "I'm *schmaert*, and I bet I could teach her how to jump through a hoop."

Mattie wrinkled her nose. "Are you saying that I'm *dumm*?"

"Didn't say you were dumb. You're just not as smart as me."

Mattie bent down to pet Twinkles, because the little

terrier had dropped the ball at her feet again. "You're full of *hochmut*, Mark. Besides, it's not nice to brag."

"I am not full of pride. I'm tellin' the truth, so it's okay to say that." Mark shoved his newly found rocks into his pockets and hurried to the house.

Mattie watched as Mark went inside. "He's full of hochmut, even if what he said was true," she mumbled to Twinkles, although she knew the dog didn't understand. Twinkles was a smart dog, though, and Mattie hoped she could teach her a lot more tricks. Maybe someday the dog would learn to jump through a hoop, but Mattie wanted to be the one who would teach her. Truth was, Mark didn't even like dogs that much. He preferred taking care of his cats. So Mattie didn't understand why he'd want to try teaching Twinkles a new trick. *Probably just to show how schmaert he is,* she thought.

Arf! Arf! Twinkles jumped up and pawed at Mattie's leg.

"Get down, Twinkles! You're getting my dress dirty," Mattie scolded when the pooch kept jumping up.

Woof! Twinkles got down and nudged the ball with her nose.

"Okay, here ya go!" Mattie leaned over, grabbed the ball, and threw it as hard as she could. The ball hit the side of the barn and bounced off, sending it far across the yard.

The dog raced after the ball, grabbed it in her mouth, and took off like a flash. Around and around the yard she went, lickety-split, as if showing off a proud possession.

"Come back with that ball!" Mattie shouted, lunging for Twinkles to try and catch her.

Twinkles kept running and didn't look back.

"Twinkles, you can sure run fast," Mattie panted. "Wish I had your energy to run like that." Truth was, Mattie could run pretty fast, and that was one of the reasons she enjoyed playing baseball so much. She played ball as good as most of the boys at school, and they liked having her on their team. Mark had never been able to run as fast as Mattie, and he wasn't good at throwing or catching the ball, either. But then, some things Mark did Mattie couldn't do as well, like spelling and thinking of big words to say. So they both had things to brag about. Of course, Mom and Dad had told the twins many times that it was wrong to boast and that bragging was a form of pride. Mattie didn't mean to be prideful, but it made her feel good to be able to do some things better than Mark, especially since he could do so many things well.

Glancing at the golden daffodils blooming across the yard, Mattie forgot about Twinkles for the time being and knelt on the grass beside her own special garden spot. Flowers seemed to be blooming everywhere. All their bright colors made Mattie think of a pretty rainbow. *Maybe I should pick a few and give them to Mom to put in a vase,* she thought. *They sure would look nice in the middle of our table at supper tonight.*

Mattie was about to pick one of the daffodils, when her brother Perry, who had recently turned six, came out of the barn, pulling his little red wagon. "Want to help me pick some flowers?" she called.

Perry shook his blond head. "I'm busy right now."

"Doing what?" Mattie asked.

"I'm gonna look for felse and load 'em into my wagon."

Mattie's eyebrows lifted. "What are ya gonna do with a bunch of rocks?"

"I'm startin' a rock collection, same as Mark." Perry looked over at her and grinned. "If I fill the whole wagon with felse, I'll have more than him."

Mattie clicked her tongue, the way Mom often did when she was trying to make a point. "That's *eefeldich*," she said with a shake of her head.

"It ain't silly." Perry gestured to a pile of rocks near the fence. "Those are bigger felse than Mark has, too."

"The word is *isn't*, not *ain't*, and it doesn't matter whose rocks are the biggest. Besides, Mark doesn't collect rocks for their size. He looks for pretty or unusual stones to add to his collection."

"I don't care," Perry argued. "I'm lookin' for the biggest ones I can find." With that, he pulled his wagon over to the fence and began loading it with rocks.

"Be careful not to scare the bluebirds nesting in the

box," Mattie warned. She was going to say more, but Twinkles showed up and dropped the ball by her knees. "Well, it's about time. Where have you been anyways?"

Twinkles tipped her head to one side and wagged her little tail. *Yip! Yip!*

Mattie picked up the ball and stood. She waited a few minutes, and laughed when Twinkles whined and pawed at her leg. Taking aim, Mattie threw the ball as hard as she could.

Whoosh! Mattie watched in horror as it sailed across the yard and right through the window on the side of the barn with a *crash*!

"Oh, no!" Mattie slapped the palm of her hand against her forehead, staring at the broken glass that lay in the grass. "Why'd this have to happen to me? I made a big mistake when I threw that ball."

Broken Glass

"What happened? How come ya broke the barn window?" Perry asked, leaving his wagon and rushing over to Mattie.

She blinked several times, trying hard not to cry. "I. . .I didn't mean to do it." Looking at what was left of the window, when only minutes ago she'd been playing fetch with her dog, Mattie wished she could rewind time and change what had happened.

"What was that?" Mark called from the back door. "I was just gettin' ready to come back outside, when I heard a loud crash."

Mattie pointed to the barn. "I threw the ball for Twinkles, but it hit the window, and now it's broke." Tears pooled in her eyes and ran down her cheeks, in spite of her best efforts to stop them. "I wonder what Mom and Dad are gonna say when they find out what I did."

Mark joined Mattie on the lawn and gave her a hug. "Don't cry. You didn't do it on purpose, and I'm sure our folks will understand."

"Sure hope you're right about that." Mattie sighed, worried about how she was going to explain all of this. "By the way, where is Mom? Did she hear the crash, too?"

"I don't think so," Mark said. "She's down in the basement, washing another load of clothes."

Mattie sank to her knees and sobbed. "That's just great. Mom will be out here soon to hang the clean clothes on the line, and then she'll see the broken window herself."

"Calm down, Mattie." Mark gently patted her back. "You're gettin' all worked up, and it won't change the fact that the window's broke."

She sniffed deeply and dried her eyes with the sleeve of her long brown dress. "Guess I shouldn't have thrown the ball so hard. My aim was way off, too."

"I'll help you clean up the glass, and then you'd better go tell Mom what happened," Mark said.

Mattie's jaw clenched. "Do I have to tell her?"

" 'Course you do. Like you said—she'll probably see it when she comes outside, so you may as well tell her now, don't ya think?"

Mattie slowly nodded. As much as she didn't want to admit what had happened, she needed to tell Mom about the broken window. "*Danki* for saying you'd help me clean up the mess," Mattie told Mark.

He smiled and rubbed Mattie's shoulder. "You're welcome. I'm going to the barn to get a cardboard box for the broken glass."

Mattie looked at Perry, who stood staring down at the pieces of broken glass. “Don’t touch,” she warned. “It’s sharp, and you could get cut.”

“I ain’t gonna touch nothin’,” Perry said with a shake of his head.

“I’m not,” Mattie corrected.

“Me neither.” Perry squinted at Mattie. “Just said that.”

She squinted back at him. “I was reminding you to say ‘I’m not,’ instead of ‘ain’t.’”

“Oh, sorry,” he mumbled, putting his hand over his mouth.

Mattie couldn’t believe her little brother couldn’t seem to remember not to say *ain’t*. Maybe he would do better once he started school in the fall. Their teacher, Anna Ruth, would never allow any of her scholars to say *ain’t*.

Thinking about school caused Mattie to remember that next Friday was their last day of classes for the late spring and summer months. Mattie was excited about that, because she and her brothers Mark and Calvin would have more time to enjoy doing many fun things they couldn’t do when they were in school all day. They would still have chores, of course, but at least Mattie could do things she enjoyed, like working in her garden, picking flowers, riding her bike, and spending time with her best friend, Stella.

Of course, being able to enjoy the beginning of school vacation depended on what her punishment might be for breaking the barn window. She might have to put fun stuff on hold for a while, especially if she had to do extra chores to pay for a new window.

Glancing up, Mattie saw a bluebird sitting in one of the big trees shading their backyard. It didn't stay there long and quickly flew over to the top of the bird box, when it started to chirp. Then another bluebird stuck its head out and flew to the roof of the barn. Mattie figured it was probably the female and had been sitting on her nest. She looked back and caught a glimpse of the other bluebird as it disappeared inside the birdhouse. "Sure wish I was one of those birds," she murmured to herself. "At least they don't have to worry about getting in trouble with their parents for throwing balls in the wrong direction."

"I'll put the broken glass in this," Mark said, returning from the barn with a small cardboard box. He squatted down on the grass and began picking up pieces of glass. "By the way, who were you talking to just now, Mattie?"

"No one but myself. I was watching the bluebirds go in and out of the birdhouse by the fence. Be careful, Mark," Mattie cautioned, turning her attention back to what he was doing. "You should wear gloves when you handle broken glass."

"I'll be fine." Mark picked up another piece and winced, dropping it suddenly. "Ouch! I cut myself!"

Mattie's eyes widened when she saw blood seeping out of Mark's thumb. "Is it bad? Should I go get Mom?"

"I think she oughta check it," Mark replied, grasping his thumb.

"I'll go get her!" Perry ran off toward the house before Mattie could make a move. A few minutes later, he was back, and Mom was with him, holding a towel.

"What happened?" Mom asked, looking at Mark with obvious concern. "Perry said you cut your finger."

"It was my thumb." Mark held up his hand.

"It doesn't look serious and should be fine with some antiseptic and a bandage," Mom said, after she'd examined Mark's thumb and wrapped it in the towel. "How did this happen?"

"I cut it on some glass," he explained, pointing to the remaining pieces lying near them, glistening in the sunlight.

Mom clicked her tongue. "How did broken glass get here on the lawn?"

"I was tossing the little red ball to Twinkles and it hit the barn window and broke the glass," Mattie said, dropping her gaze to the ground. "I'm sorry, Mom. Do you think Dad will be upset with me? Guess my aim was off, but I didn't do it on purpose."

"I believe he will understand, Mattie," Mom said, looking at where the glass in the opening of the window had been. "He has some spare glass in the barn, so he should be able to fix the window. However, you do need to be more careful when you're throwing a ball outside. Keep it away from the barn and the house."

Mattie bobbed her head. "I know, and I'll try not to let it happen again."

Mom smiled and gave Mattie a hug. Then she turned to Mark and said, "Let's get you inside now so I can clean your thumb and put a bandage on the cut."

"What about the broken glass?" he asked. "It still needs to be picked up and thrown away."

"Just leave it for now. I'll tend to it after I take care of your thumb." Mom motioned to Perry, who stood nearby. "You'd better come inside with me. I don't want you anywhere near that broken glass."

As Mom, Mark, and Perry started for the house, Mattie breathed a sigh of relief. She was thankful she wasn't in trouble for breaking the window and grateful that Mom had been so understanding about it. Hopefully Dad would be, too. Right now, though, Mattie needed to get Twinkles and take her into the house so she didn't go near the glass and get her little paws cut.

"How is your thumb feeling, Son?" Mom asked as Mark sat at the table eating supper with his family.

"It's okay," Mark replied, reaching around the vase Mattie had filled with flowers, for a piece of Mom's tasty meat loaf. Truth was, his thumb throbbed a bit, but he wouldn't admit it—especially with his little brother, Perry, sitting beside him. Mark wanted Perry, as well as his older brothers, Calvin, Russell, and Ike, to think he was brave. After all, he would be ten years old in four months, and that meant he was growing up. Mark was getting taller, too, and that made him happy. For the longest time, Mattie had been taller than him, and now they were nearly the same height.

"Next time you need to pick up broken glass, you should put on a pair of gloves," Dad said, fingering his full blond beard that matched the color of his hair.

"Jah, I know," Mark said with a nod. "I didn't think about looking for my gloves, but I'll be more careful from now on." He glanced at Mattie and figured from her relaxed expression that she was glad Dad hadn't gotten upset about her breaking the window. He, like Mom, had given Mattie a lecture about staying clear of windows when playing with a ball.

"Accidents can happen so quickly, and we all need to use caution when we're doing things." Dad looked across the table at seventeen-year-old Ike. "Remember the other day when you were cutting some pieces of wood in my shop?"

Ike nodded slowly and brushed a piece of auburn hair out of his eyes. "If I hadn't been watching what I was doing, I could have cut my fingers on the saw."

Mark clenched his teeth. His thumb felt bad enough from being cut by glass. He couldn't imagine how much pain he would feel if he'd gotten cut by a saw.

"I think we should talk about something else." Mom turned to Calvin. "How did things go for you and

Russell today, when you went to help Grandpa Miller chop and stack firewood from that tree he cut down?"

"Went real well." Calvin, who was twelve, bobbed his blond head. "Grandpa paid us when we were done."

"And Grandma fed us a big lunch, with chocolate cupcakes for dessert," Russell put in. He was fifteen and worked in Dad's shop with Ike part-time.

"Did ya bring some home for us to eat?" Perry asked with an eager expression. "I love cupcakes!"

"Nope. Sorry, but we ate them all," Calvin said.

"How about a piece of strawberry pie?" Mom nodded toward two pies sitting on the counter. "That's what I made for our dessert tonight, using some of the berries I froze last summer."

Perry smacked his lips. "Yum!"

"Yum! Yum!" four-year-old Ada repeated; then she giggled and clapped her hands, like she always did when she got excited. Ada also had red hair, just like the twins'.

"What about the rest of you?" Mom took a drink of water. "Does strawberry pie sound good to you?"

Mark and Mattie both nodded, and so did Dad, Calvin, Russell, and Ike.

Mom smiled. "All right then, it's strawberry pie for everyone."

After the meal was finished, Mom dished up the mouth-watering pie and handed each person a tall wedge on their plate.

"This is *appeditlich*," Mattie said after she'd taken her first bite. "I love sweet strawberries—in a pie, over ice cream, or just in a bowl by themselves."

"Mattie's right," Dad agreed. "The pie is delicious."

The rest of the family bobbed their heads in agreement—even little Ada, with strawberry juice rolling down her chin.

When they were done eating, Mark announced that he was going out to the barn to feed his cats.

"Can I go with ya, Mark?" Perry asked.

"Sure," Mark replied. He thought it was nice that his little brother liked to be with him. In fact, Mark felt kind of proud about this. It meant that Perry looked up to him, the way Mark did with his oldest brother, Ike.

"Before you go," Mom said, "I'm wondering if you've studied your spelling words for the test you'll be having on Monday."

Mark shook his head. "Don't need to study 'cause I already know all the words."

"You shouldn't be bragging like that," Mattie said, bumping Mark's arm with her elbow.

"I'm not bragging. It's a fact." Mark jiggled his eyebrows up and down. "Just wait till Monday, and you'll see what a good grade I get on the spelling test."

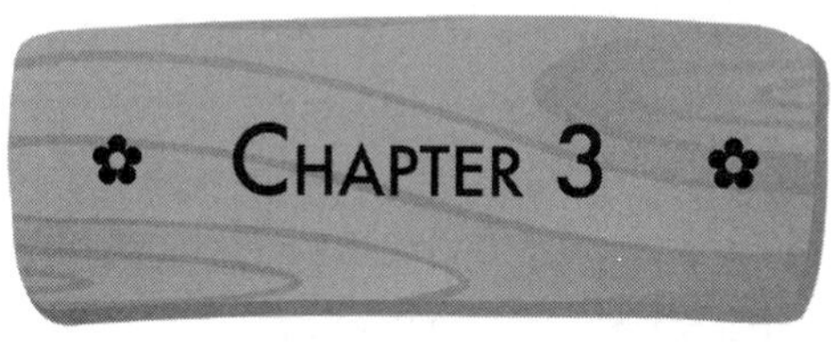

Chapter 3

Found with the Trash

"Should we ride our bicycle-built-for-two today?" Mark asked Mattie on Monday morning after they'd finished eating breakfast. "Sometimes I like it better than riding our own bikes to school 'cause we can visit easier if we're closer together."

"That's fine with me," Mattie said, scooping her backpack and lunch pail off the kitchen counter.

The twins hugged Mom good-bye and hurried out the back door. Their older brother Calvin was ahead of them on his bike, but Mark didn't care. He and Mattie still had plenty of time to get to school, even if they made a quick stop along the way. Mark enjoyed scouting for things on their route that he could fix up and reuse.

"Hope I do well on the spelling test our teacher gives us today," Mattie said as she climbed on their bike behind Mark. "I studied all the words this weekend, and some of them are hard."

"Not for me." Mark started pedaling, and Mattie

did the same. He laughed as they left their yard and the gentle wind blew in his face. It was a warm breeze, and the intense blue sky overhead was cloudless. If they didn't have to go to school today, it would be a great day for fishing. Mark looked forward to this summer, when he and Grandpa Miller could go fishing and relax at the pond near their home. He was also anxious to spend time with his best friend, John Schrock, and thought it would be fun if they went camping with their dads this year. Of course, his brothers would probably want to go along, because they liked camping as much as Mark did.

"How's your thumb doing?" Mattie asked.

"Not too bad. It throbbed at first but feels much better now."

They rode in silence for a while. Mark saw a lot of different rocks, and he would have liked to stop and take a closer look, but they could do that on their way home from school. Mark spotted a group of stones that really sparkled, and he paid close attention to where they were so he could find them later. Luckily, the stones were near a fence post at the edge of a field. Mark figured he'd soon need another box to keep his rock collection in. Maybe at supper tonight he'd ask Dad if there was any extra lumber in the barn and if he would have time to make a big, sturdy box for Mark's growing collection. One large wooden box would be better than several smaller boxes pushed under his bed. Maybe he could keep the bigger box in the barn or even in their buggy shed.

As they continued on, Mark realized he was pedaling to the rhythm of a tune Mattie was humming. He recognized the song but couldn't remember the name of it. Just as he was about to ask his sister what the melody was, Mattie stopped humming and shouted, "Hey, look over there!"

Mark's gaze went to the left. "Where? I don't see anything unusual over there."

"No, not that side. Look to your right." Mattie giggled. "I see a bunch of wildflowers blooming. Think they might be buttercups mixed in with all those blue violets. Maybe we can stop after school and pick some for Mom."

"We'll see about that," Mark replied. "If we have time, that is. I saw some sparkly rocks back there by the field, and I'd like to stop on our way home this afternoon and get 'em."

"How about this? We can park our bike between both places. While I pick flowers, you can gather the rocks. You can't take too many, though, 'cause there's not much room in our bicycle basket," Mattie said.

Now that Mark had something to look forward to, he started whistling to the melody Mattie had been humming. As they approached their neighbor's house, Mark quit pedaling and pulled back on the brake handle.

Mattie tapped Mark's shoulder. "Why are we stopping?"

"I see the Johnsons' garbage out by the road, and I

want to see if they're getting rid of anything I might want."

"Oh, no. Not this again." Mattie groaned. "Just because they gave you that old bike awhile back, doesn't mean you should pick up everything they've set by the side of the road for the trash collector."

"I don't want everything; only the good stuff I might be able to use." Mark got off the bike and left his sister holding on to it. He walked over to see what was in the Johnsons' trash. "Looks like there's a basketball hoop they don't want anymore," he called to Mattie.

She set the kickstand on their bike and came over to join him. "Jah, that's what it looks like, all right, but its old and rusty, and the netting's gone."

"I don't care. I'm gonna ask if I can take it."

Mattie rolled her eyes. "What do you want with a rusty old basketball hoop?"

"I'm gonna clean it up, and then I'll ask Dad or Ike to help me hang it on the side of the barn so I can shoot some baskets." Mark grinned. "If I practice real hard, bet I can make more baskets than any of my brothers."

"I'll bet ya can't, 'cause you don't even have a basketball to go with the hoop. Besides, I think any of our brothers, except maybe Perry, who's not so tall, can play basketball better than you."

Mark shrugged his shoulders. "We'll see about that." He picked up the hoop, stepped onto the Johnsons' back porch, and knocked on the door. Soon, he heard the steady rhythm of feet approaching the door. A few seconds later, Mrs. Johnson answered Mark's knock.

"Well, if it isn't Mark Miller," she said, smiling. "What can I do for you this morning?"

Mark held up the basketball hoop. "I noticed that you'd thrown this out with the trash, and I was wondering if I could have it." His darting gaze joined the object he held.

She nodded quickly. "That's not a problem at all. Just leave it on the porch and stop back for it on your way home from school. I hope you can clean it up and have a lot of fun playing basketball, like our kids used to do."

"Thank you very much." Whistling, Mark set the hoop down and headed back to where Mattie stood waiting near their bike.

"What did Mrs. Johnson say, and where's the old hoop?" Mattie asked, tapping her foot against the pavement.

"She said I could have it and that she'll hold it for me till we stop back here on our way home from school." Mark could hardly wait to clean up the old hoop. Better yet, he looked forward to practicing, so he could show everyone how good he was.

As Mattie sat at her school desk that morning, she thought about the basketball hoop Mark had discovered by the Johnsons' trash. She didn't understand why her brother wanted it so badly, because he didn't even have a basketball. What good was a hoop without a ball? Maybe he planned to save his money and buy a ball, but that could take awhile, because neither of the twins had done anything to earn money for some time. They would make some money once their family's produce stand was set up at the end of their driveway near the road, but that wouldn't be until summer, which was more than a month away.

Maybe Mark will ask Grandpa or Dad if they have some work he can do to make money, Mattie thought. *That's what I would do if I wanted to buy something new.*

Their teacher, Anna Ruth, announced that it was time for the spelling test, bringing Mattie's thoughts to a halt.

Mattie looked over at Mark, whose desk was across from hers, and couldn't help but notice his big smile. Spelling, like most other subjects they learned in school, came easy to her twin. Even though he hadn't studied for the test, she figured he would do well because he was so smart.

I studied hard for this test, so I hope I'll do well, too, she thought.

"Does everyone have their paper and pencils ready?" Anna Ruth asked the class.

All heads bobbed up and down.

"All right then. Let's begin. The first word is *excited.*" Their teacher paused. "Did everyone get that?"

Most of the children nodded, including Mattie, but

Mark raised his hand. "I don't remember that word being on the list you gave us on Friday," he said, after Anna Ruth called on him.

"Yes, it was," their teacher replied.

Mark opened his mouth, as though he might say something more, but then he closed it and wrote the word on his paper.

Since Mark hadn't studied the spelling words, Mattie figured he'd probably forgotten what some of them were. Since Mattie had studied the words for the test, she remembered how to spell this first one.

"Now for the second word," Anna Ruth said, smiling at the scholars as she stood near her desk holding the list of words. "It's *balloon*."

Mark's hand shot up again. "I'm sure that word wasn't on the list you gave us last Friday," he said, frowning.

"Yes, Mark, it was on the list, too." Anna Ruth said.

Several others nodded in agreement, and so did Mattie. She remembered the word well, because it made her think of the red balloon Mom had bought for Ada the last time they'd gone shopping at one of the stores in Millersburg.

Mark scratched the side of his head and pursed his lips as he wrote the second word on his paper.

Mattie figured he was wishing now that he'd studied for the spelling test instead of thinking he knew the words already. She wondered if he might even fail the test. *Maybe he would learn a lesson if he did,* she thought. *He's always telling me I ought to study more, so now maybe Mark will realize that he should always study for any test.*

Mark's palms grew sweaty, and his mouth felt dry as cardboard. The spelling words Anna Ruth gave them weren't the ones he thought they'd be given. He wondered if he had taken home the wrong list. Mark was sure he'd copied them down correctly after Anna Ruth wrote them on the blackboard Friday afternoon, but maybe the paper he took home had been the one from the previous week. Since their teacher gave them words to study each week from the list she wrote on the blackboard, it could have easily happened that he'd taken the wrong words home.

Guess that's what I get for not looking at the list right away, he thought. *If I don't know all the words Teacher gives us today, I'll probably fail this spelling test. I should have dated each of my word lists, and then this wouldn't have happened. If Mattie does well on the test, I bet she'll be the one bragging.*

Mark did the best he could with all the words Anna Ruth gave them and was glad he knew at least some of them. A few, like the word *balloon*, he wasn't too sure about. Did it have two *l*'s or one? Was there an *e* at the end of the word? Mark knew he wouldn't find out how well he'd done until they got to school tomorrow, so he would just try not to think about it. All he wanted to concentrate on was school getting over for the day so he could stop at the Johnsons' and get that basketball hoop. Mark wasn't interested anymore in stopping for the sparkly rocks he'd seen; at least not today. He hoped Mattie had forgotten about the wildflowers she wanted to pick. Maybe tomorrow after school, they could stop for both.

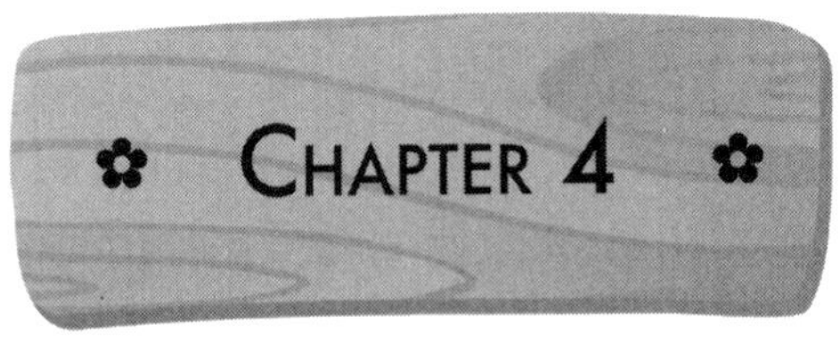

Test Results

"Hey, Mom, guess what I found on the way to school this morning!" Mark announced when he and Mattie arrived home from school.

Mom turned from the sink, where she was washing a head of lettuce, and smiled. "What did you find, Son?"

"Found an old basketball hoop," he replied with a grin. "It was sittin' out with the Johnsons' trash, and Mrs. Johnson said I could have it. Mattie and I stopped after school to get it, and I slipped it over the handlebars on our bike so I could bring it home."

Mom's pale eyebrows rose high on her forehead. "But why would you want an old hoop? You don't even have a basketball, Mark."

"I know, but I'm gonna save up my money and buy one as soon as I can. Then after I get the hoop cleaned up, I'm gonna ask Dad or Ike if they'll hang it on the side of the barn where there are no *fenschdere*."

"That's good," Mom said, "because we don't need any more broken windows." She motioned to the bowl of fruit on the table. "Why don't you two have a snack? Dad, Ike, and Russell have to work a little longer than usual in the woodshop today, so I won't serve supper until seven."

"Danki, Mom." Mattie grabbed a banana, and Mark took an apple. "What are we havin' for supper tonight?" Mattie asked.

"I'm fixing chicken and dumplings and a big tossed green salad," Mom responded.

Mattie licked her lips. "Yum. I love chicken and dumplings."

"How was school today?" Mom asked. "Did you both do well on the spelling test?"

"I hope so," Mattie said, taking a seat at the table. "Some of the words were hard, but since I studied them real good, I think I may have done okay. We won't get our test scores till tomorrow, though."

Mom looked at Mark. "How about you? Did you think the words were difficult?"

Mark didn't want to admit that he'd had trouble with the spelling words, so he merely shrugged and said, "They were different than I thought they'd be, but hopefully, I did okay."

"You should have studied," Mattie said, peeling her banana and taking a bite.

"Wouldn't have mattered if I had." Mark grunted. "I brought the wrong list of words home with me on Friday. Think I picked up the list from the week before by mistake."

"If you had looked at the list when you got home, you would have realized it wasn't the right one." Mom clicked her tongue. "Next time, you'd better pay closer attention."

Mark nodded. "Jah, I know."

"I had the right list of spelling words," Mattie said. "So you could have borrowed mine."

Mark nodded again. Then he looked back at Mom and said, "Say, where's Calvin? Since Mattie and I stopped at the Johnsons' to pick up the basketball hoop, I figured our *bruder* would be here by now."

"Your brother went over to Grandpa and Grandma Millers' house to do some more chores for Grandpa," Mom said, taking a seat at the table across from the twins. "I believe he'll stay there for supper."

Mark frowned. If Calvin was doing chores for Grandpa, he would no doubt get paid. Mark wished he'd been asked to go along, because he could sure use the money.

Mattie finished eating her banana and put the peeling in the garbage can under the sink. "Is it okay if I go outside to play?" she asked. "I want to work with Twinkles on a new trick."

"That's fine," Mom said. "Just be sure to change out of your school clothes first. And if you have any homework, you'll need to get that done before you play. Oh, and you and Mark have some clean clothes on your beds that need to be put away." She smiled and helped herself to an orange.

"Anna Ruth didn't give us homework today," Mark

announced. "So I guess we can both go out to play after we've put our laundry away." He finished his apple, tossed the core in the garbage, and raced upstairs to change his clothes. If he got outside before Mattie, maybe he could surprise her by teaching Twinkles a really good trick, because a great idea had just popped into his head.

"Where's Twinkles?" Mattie asked Mom when she came downstairs with the dog's brush. "I want to comb her hair before I work with her on a trick. When I went upstairs, she was in the living room, sleeping on the floor beside Perry."

"Perry's asleep?" Mom's fingers touched her parted lips. "The little fellow was playing hard today and must have worn himself out. I know Ada's tired, because when I put her down for a nap earlier, she fell asleep within minutes."

"But what about Twinkles?" Mattie questioned. "Have you seen her, Mom?"

Mom nodded. "She went outside with Mark."

Mattie's forehead wrinkled. "Why would he take my dog outside?"

"He said something about teaching her a special trick."

"Humph!" Mattie put both hands on her hips. "Twinkles is my dog, and if anyone's gonna teach her new tricks, it oughta be me." She hurried outside, making sure the door didn't slam behind her.

After looking around the yard for a bit, and seeing no sign of her dog, Mattie made her way to the barn. Stepping inside, she halted, shocked by what she saw. Mark held that rusty old basketball hoop and was trying to coax Twinkles to jump through it.

"*Absatz!*" she shouted. "You need to stop what you're doing right now!"

Mark turned and looked at Mattie like she had said something horrible. "Don't shout like that. You're gonna scare Twinkles, and then she'll never jump through this hoop."

Mattie marched over to Mark. "I'm the one who should be teaching her new tricks. She knows me best and does what I say."

"All right then," Mark said. "Try to get her to jump through this hoop."

Mattie shook her head. "That old hoop is rusty, and besides, I think it's too small for Twinkles to jump through, because it's even smaller than my Hula-Hoop, and she wouldn't jump through that." She bent down and picked up her dog.

"Aw, Mattie, I just wanted to have a little fun."

"I don't call that fun. Besides, I think you should forget about trying to fix up that old hoop. I don't see how you'll ever make it look halfway decent—especially when the netting's missing. What will you use to replace it?" Mattie questioned.

"Don't know yet," Mark replied. "I'll find something to fix it, and when I'm done, it'll look brand new."

"If you ask me, it would have been better if you'd left the hoop at the Johnsons' and we'd stopped after school so I could pick wildflowers and you could get those sparkly rocks you'd seen." Mattie headed out of the barn. "Come on, Twinkles. I'm gonna take you back to the house and sit in the utility room to comb your hair till it's nice and shiny."

When Mattie entered the kitchen with Twinkles, Perry came in, rubbing his eyes. "There's a puddle of water on the living-room floor, and I stepped in it," he complained, wrinkling his nose.

"Where is it?" Mattie asked. "Show me."

Perry led the way. "It's right there." He pointed at a yellowish liquid spot.

Mattie groaned, knowing this was Twinkles's fault.

Just then, Mom came into the room, carrying rosy-cheeked Ada. "Mattie, I thought you'd gone outside to play."

"I did, but Mark upset me, so I came in with Twinkles." Mattie pointed to the puddle on the floor. "Guess my dog made a mess when she was in here with Perry earlier. Sorry about this, Mom. I'll clean it up right away."

"This is why I don't like the dog to be left in the house unattended," Mom said with a huff. "She sometimes piddles, especially when she gets excited."

Mom placed Ada on the sofa and took Perry's hand. "Let's get you into the bathroom and wash your feet while your sister cleans up after Twinkles." She turned to look over her shoulder at Mattie. "Please put the dog outside so she doesn't make any more messes."

Mattie nodded. "Okay, Mom, I will."

"If Mattie hadn't come in when she did, I would've had Twinkles jumping through this hoop," Mark mumbled, after he'd been sitting in the barn for some time, petting his cats, Boots and Lucky. "And I'll bet Mattie's gonna be mighty surprised when she sees how the old basketball hoop looks after it's fixed up. I'm sure Grandpa Miller has an old fishing net around that I could use for the netting."

"Are you talking to yourself?"

Mark jumped at the sound of his brother's voice. "Russell, don't sneak up on me like that."

"I wasn't sneakin'." Russell chuckled. "You're awful jumpy, Mark."

"I didn't expect you to come into the barn right now," Mark said. "Thought you and Ike were workin' in Dad's shop today."

"We were, but Dad said he didn't need my help anymore, so I came on up to the house to do our chores and get washed for supper." Russell motioned to the basketball hoop Mark held. "Say, where did you get that?"

Mark explained how he'd found the hoop, and ended by saying that he wouldn't be able to use it until he got some money saved up to buy a ball.

"Think I can help you with that," Russell said. "I've saved some of the money I've earned helping in Dad's shop, and Calvin's earning money helping Grandpa this afternoon, so maybe the two of us can chip in on the basketball. Then we can all three play the game."

"That's a great idea. Danki, Russell." Mark smiled widely. "In the meantime, I'm gonna try to clean it up, spray it with some of Dad's paint, and then I'll ask Grandpa if he has some old fishing net. Think it'd make a good replacement for the netting that's missing. What do you think?"

"That'd probably work pretty well. It's good you thought of it," Russell said, clasping Mark's shoulder.

Mark grinned. He could hardly wait until they bought the basketball.

After Mattie cleaned up Twinkles's mess and brushed the dog's hair, she decided to head back outside and see how the flowers in her little garden were doing. Maybe later she would work with Twinkles on a new trick. Right now, she was upset with her pooch.

The crocuses Mattie planted last fall had been the first flowers to bloom earlier in the spring. She'd forgotten how many bulbs she had covered with dirt and was happy when so many appeared. Some were dark purple, others white, and even some yellow. Soon after that, Mattie's daffodils had bloomed, and now her tulips were ready to open. When that happened, she wanted to pick a few of them for Mom to put in a vase. These tulips smelled so good and would look pretty as a centerpiece on the table. Mattie was proud of her flower bed. It actually seemed to be doing better than Mom's.

Mattie bent down to pull a few weeds that had popped up in some areas of her garden, when all of a sudden she saw a flash of brown off to the right.

"What was that?" she said, looking in that direction. Then she saw it. "Now where did you come from?" Mattie reached over and picked up the tiny baby bunny that must have been sitting there the whole time, unseen. She quickly forgot about the weeds she wanted to pull. Holding the furry bunny tenderly in the cup of her hand, she watched as its cute little whiskered nose wiggled.

"Do you have a nest nearby, little one?" Mattie spoke softly, while petting the bunny's small head. "Maybe I can find it for you." She sat a little longer, enjoying the feel of the baby rabbit in her hand. The little creature was so small and most likely felt frightened, but it seemed to relax in the warmth of Mattie's hand. After a few minutes, the rabbit closed its eyes.

"I'd sure like to keep you, but I know it wouldn't be right," Mattie whispered, stroking the bunny's soft fur.

"If your nest is somewhere nearby, maybe I can watch you grow throughout the summer."

Mattie continued to hold the little rabbit as she looked all around. Then she noticed a small indentation in the ground where her "Mattie's Corner" sign hung. A closer look revealed where the bunny nest was, and she could see more tiny noses at the entrance.

"In you go with your brothers and sisters." Mattie smiled as she gently placed the bunny back in the hole with the other baby bunnies. She saw that the small hole had been lined with rabbit fur, most likely from the mother rabbit when she was building the nest.

She stood and ran toward the barn, anxious to tell Mark about her find. She hoped that neither his cats nor her dog would discover the rabbit nest, because she didn't want them to frighten or hurt the baby bunnies.

No Fun Jumping Rope

"Watch out, Mattie. You spilled some milk on the floor," Mom said as Mattie carried over to the sink what was left of the milk in her cereal bowl.

"Oops! Sorry about that." Mattie pulled a paper towel from the roll on the counter and dropped it on the floor so it covered the milk. Then she opened the back door and called her dog. A few minutes later, Twinkles raced into the kitchen. *Arf! Arf!*

"Clean it up," Mattie said, pointing to the paper towel.

Twinkles looked up at Mattie and tipped her little brown-and-white head. Had she already forgotten the trick Mattie had taught her?

"What are you doing?" Mom asked, her eyebrows pulling together.

"Watch this. Twinkles has learned a new trick." Mattie snapped her fingers and pointed once more.

Twinkles put one paw on the paper towel and moved it back and forth.

Mattie smiled and nodded; Mom gasped; Mark

rolled his eyes; Ada squealed, while clapping her hands; and the rest of Mattie's family looked on in surprise.

"Now that's some trick," Dad said, chuckling. "How'd you get the dog to do that, Mattie?"

"After Twinkles piddled on the floor yesterday, I decided to teach her how to clean up after herself," Mattie replied, feeling rather proud.

Mom slowly shook her head. "It's a good trick you taught your *hund*, but I'd prefer that she didn't make messes in the house at all. I don't know why Twinkles isn't completely housebroken by now, but unless someone is with your dog, watching her all the time, I think she should stay outside."

Mattie frowned. "But Mom, that's not fair. Twinkles is a good dog, and—"

"Sometimes she makes messes," Mark spoke up.

"Your *mamm* is right," Dad interjected. "We can't let Twinkles roam all over the house unless she's watched closely so she won't get excited and have an accident."

"You should have taught her to scratch on the door or bark when she needs to go outside, rather than teaching her how to clean up after she makes a mess," Mark said.

"Mark is right," Mom agreed, "but I'll have to admit, Mattie, that was a pretty good trick you taught your hund. Regardless, Twinkles is not to be left in the house alone. Is that understood?"

"I'll watch her whenever she's inside, and I'll

work on teaching her what Mark suggested," Mattie promised. "It shouldn't take real long, either, 'cause I'm a good teacher and Twinkles learns fast."

"That's good to hear." Dad pushed away from the table. "Now it's time for each of us to get on with our day."

Mark dreaded going to school today, because he was worried about how he'd done on yesterday's spelling test. But he had to go, and so did Mattie and Calvin. Mark hoped he was wrong and had spelled a lot of the words correctly, but he had a feeling he'd be facing the consequences of not studying the correct ones.

Today, they were riding their own bikes to school, and Calvin rode up ahead. Mark thought about the sparkly rocks he'd seen yesterday. On the way home from school, he was going to stop and get some of those pretty stones. Mark had even brought a small box along, which he carried in his bicycle basket, so he could get the rocks home. He still needed to talk to Dad about getting some wood to make a bigger storage box for all of his rocks.

The morning started out nice and sunny, and it grew warmer as they got closer to school. Mark almost stopped to take off his jacket but decided to keep on pedaling. It would be a great day for recess when they went outside for lunch later on.

As they rode farther, Mark started thinking about

the trick Mattie had taught her dog. He had to admit, it was pretty amazing to watch Twinkles use her paw that way. Mark would love to be able to teach one of his cats a unique trick—something even better than what Twinkles could do. *Maybe I can work on that once school is out*, he decided. *I'll show Mattie that my* katze *are even smarter than her hund.*

Mark glanced over his shoulder at Mattie, riding several feet behind on her bike. *I wonder if she'll stop and pick some wildflowers on the way home. Knowing my twin sister, I'll bet she does.* Calvin, riding his bike, was still up ahead, but Mark didn't mind about that at all.

When the schoolhouse came into view, Mark's thoughts turned to the spelling test again. In some ways he hoped Anna Ruth wouldn't hand out their papers until the end of the day. But if she waited, he'd have all day to worry about it, and that might be even worse. So maybe it would be best if he found out first off how he'd done on the test.

After Mark and Mattie pulled into the school yard and parked their bikes near the others, Mark spotted his friend John across the yard and hurried over to talk to him. "Guess what I found yesterday?" he asked.

"I don't know," John said. "Seems like you're always finding something."

Mark grinned. "Found an old basketball hoop in front of the Johnsons' place, and Mrs. Johnson said I could keep it."

"That's great. Have you used it yet?" John questioned.

Mark shook his head. "It's kind of rusty and needs to be cleaned and painted. It also needs a new net, but I'm hoping Grandpa Miller can help with that. Oh, and Calvin and Russell are going to help me buy a basketball so we can all play."

"Sounds like fun," John said. "Think I'll be able to come over to your house and play basketball, too?"

"Don't see why not. We can take turns shootin' hoops, and it'll be lots of fun."

"Well, if ya need any help fixin' it up, just let me know."

Mark smiled. "That's nice of you, but I think my *brieder* are gonna help me clean it up, and I'll ask Grandpa Miller about makin' a new net for the hoop."

The bell rang, calling them inside. With a feeling of dread, Mark followed his friend into the schoolhouse. Mark put his lunch box away and took a seat at his desk, just as the other scholars did. After Anna Ruth read a verse from the book of Matthew in the Bible, the children stood and recited the Lord's Prayer. Following that, everyone filed to the front of the room and sang a few songs.

When they returned to their desks, Anna Ruth handed out the graded spelling test. The older students, like Calvin, had been given a different set of words for their test, and she handed those out, too. Mark's jaw clenched when he saw that he'd missed nearly half of the words. *I'll have to do better from now on,* he told himself. Then he remembered that this Friday was their last day of school until the new term began near the end of summer. *I'll do better next year, that's for sure.*

"How'd you do on the test?" Mattie whispered from across the aisle.

Mark frowned. "Not good. I missed several words." *I wonder how Calvin did on his spelling test.*

"That's too bad," she responded. "For the first time ever I got them all right."

Mark forced a smile. "I'm sure you're glad about that."

Mattie nodded.

I'm happy for Mattie, Mark thought. *But I wish I didn't have to go home today and tell Mom and Dad how bad I did on the test. Maybe they won't bring it up.*

Just before noon recess, Anna Ruth reminded the class that Friday was the last day of school and their families were all invited to come for the program and picnic lunch. "I know most of your mothers will bring food to share," Anna Ruth said, "but if any of you would like to bring a dessert that you bake yourself, that would be nice, too. Be sure to ask permission and get some supervision when you cook."

Mattie smiled. Maybe she would bake a special cake by herself, without any help from Mom. That would show everyone at school what a good baker she was.

In fact, my cake might be the best dessert of all, she thought.

"All right, class, you may get your lunches and go outside," Anna Ruth announced.

Mark picked up his paper and went forward to talk to Anna Ruth. Mattie waited a few minutes, hoping to hear what he said.

"I took the wrong spelling words home, and then figuring that I knew all of them, I didn't study," Mark admitted to their teacher. "Would you let me retake the test?"

"I'm sorry, Mark," Anna Ruth said, "but it wouldn't be fair to the rest of the class if I let you do that. You see, others missed several words, and if I allowed one of my scholars to retest, I'd have to do it for everyone."

Mark stood with his head down and paper held behind his back. Then he slowly nodded, turned, and headed outside.

Mattie knew her brother was disappointed, and she felt bad for him. But he should have taken his paper out and looked at the words. If he'd done so, he would have realized that he had the wrong list, and she would have let him study hers.

Knowing she couldn't help Mark, Mattie got her lunch pail and joined her friend Stella. They sat down on the porch steps, and after saying a silent prayer, Mattie took out the ham-and-cheese sandwich Mom had prepared.

"Wanna trade with me?" Stella asked, holding out her sandwich to Mattie. "My mamm made me a tuna sandwich this morning, and I don't like tuna that much."

Mattie wrinkled her nose. "Me neither. Think I'll stick with my ham and cheese."

Stella sighed. "That's okay. I don't blame ya. If I had ham and cheese and you had tuna, I wouldn't want to trade, either."

Mattie felt bad for her friend, so she offered Stella half of her sandwich. "I'm not all that *hungerich*, so I don't mind if you want this," she said.

Stella smiled and took the sandwich. "Danki, Mattie. You're such a good friend. Do you want half my tuna?"

"No thanks." Mattie gave Stella's arm a gentle squeeze. "You're a good friend, too."

"How'd you do on the spelling test?" Stella asked, after taking a bite of the ham-and-cheese sandwich.

"I got all of them right this time," Mattie said, feeling quite proud of herself. "I never got a perfect score on a spelling test before, so I guess it pays to study. How'd you do?"

"There was one word I didn't get right," Stella admitted. "I spelled the word *absence* wrong.

"That is a confusing word," Mattie said. "I'm usually not sure whether to use a *c* or an *s*."

"That's where I got hung up," Stella added. "I even wrote it down correctly the first time; then I didn't think it looked right, so I spelled it a-b-s-e-n-s-e. Oh well, don't think I'll forget how to spell that word again."

The girls visited more while they ate their lunch, and afterward, Amy Bontrager asked if they would like to join her in a game of jump rope.

Mattie bobbed her head. "I'm really good at jumping rope, and I can't wait to play. Bet I can do the most jumps of all."

A few minutes later, Mattie was jumping, while Stella held one end of the rope and Amy held the other. "Fifty-five, fifty-six, fifty-seven," Mattie panted breathlessly as she continued to jump. "I'm gonna make one hundred, just wait and see."

On and on, Mattie jumped, barely able to catch her breath but determined to keep going until she reached her goal. "Ninety-five, ninety-six, ninety-seven, ninety—"

Whoosh! Mattie's half-slip fell off her waist and dropped to the ground, causing her feet to get tangled. She tripped and fell on top of the slip. "*Ach*, no!" Mattie gasped. Her cheeks burned with shame. Not only had she missed her goal of one hundred jumps, but everyone watching had seen what happened—even some of the boys who stood nearby.

Mattie quickly grabbed her underskirt, clambered to her feet, and raced to the outhouse in tears. Hearing laughter from some of her classmates really hurt, but even with the concern she heard in Stella's voice when she called after her, Mattie didn't think she could ever face any of her friends again. She wished that she hadn't bragged about being so good.

Mattie Hides Out

"Where's your sister?" Anna Ruth asked Mark after he and the rest of the class returned to their desks when recess was over.

Mark glanced at Mattie's empty chair and shrugged his shoulders. "Don't know where she is. Thought she came in when the rest of us did."

"Mattie was jumping rope and her slip fell off, so she ran to the outhouse," Stella spoke up. "She was *umgerennt* and said she was never coming out."

"I'd be upset, too, if something like that happened to me. I'd better go check on her." Anna Ruth rose from her chair and stopped in front of Karen Yoder's desk. "Please take over for me while I'm gone," she said.

"Yes, Teacher." Karen, who was in the eighth grade and would be graduating on Friday, went to the front of the room and sat in the chair at Anna Ruth's desk.

From his seat, Mark could see out the window as their teacher hurried toward the outhouse.

Mark sighed deeply. During recess, he'd been

sitting on the fence with some other boys his age and hadn't seen what had happened to Mattie. This was not turning into a good day for either him or his twin sister.

Anxious for a breath of fresh air, Mattie opened the outhouse door and peered out. Seeing no children in the school yard, she stepped outside but remained behind the wooden partition that separated the girls' bathroom from the boys'. She had put her slip back on, even though it was bit dirty from being on the ground when she'd tripped on the jump rope and fallen. Several of the girls had seen what happened, and some had even laughed at her. A few boys nearby had snickered, too. No way could she go back inside and face her classmates. It was too embarrassing! Mattie had been so happy when she'd found out she did well on the spelling test, but now that didn't matter. All she could think about was how she wished she had never tried to out-jump her friends and the humiliation she'd felt when her slip fell off.

Mattie's friend Stella had followed her to the outhouse and tried to encourage Mattie to come out. When Stella said, "Not to worry—it could have been worse," Mattie was still too embarrassed to face any of the scholars. Even when her best friend said she'd walk back to class with her, Mattie kept hidden until Stella left.

"Wish there was a way I could sneak home so I could

get away from my hurt pride." Mattie moaned with frustration. Since she couldn't run off, Mattie stood with a heated face and watched at the top of the wooden panel as a little spider spun its web.

A few minutes later, Mattie heard footsteps, and when she peered around the partition, she saw her teacher heading toward her. *Oh, great,* Mattie thought. *I'm probably in trouble for not going back to class after recess.*

"Are you okay, Mattie?" Anna Ruth asked. "I heard about what happened to your slip and how you fell."

Tears welled in Mattie's eyes, and she blinked several times to keep them from falling onto her cheeks. "I'm not hurt, but I can't face the others who laughed when they saw what happened. I–I'm afraid they may laugh and make fun of me again."

"No, they won't," Anna Ruth said with a shake of her head. "I'll make sure of it, Mattie."

Mattie knew her teacher would do as she said, but it was still hard to make herself go back to the schoolhouse. Too bad it wasn't time to go home.

"I remember something really embarrassing that happened to me when I was a girl," Anna Ruth said.

"What was it?" Mattie asked with curiosity.

"I had gone to the outhouse during recess, and when I came back, I didn't realize it at first, but there was a strip of toilet paper stuck to my shoe, and as I walked, it dragged behind me. Of course, everyone who saw it began to laugh and point at my shoe."

"Oh, no." Mattie grimaced. "You must have been very umgerennt."

Anna Ruth nodded. "I was upset, but even though some of the scholars made fun of me, I pulled the paper free, put on a happy face, and tried to get through the rest of my day the best way I could."

Mattie wasn't sure she could put on a happy face, but she would go back to the schoolhouse and try to get through the rest of her day. She hoped nothing like what had happened today would ever happen to her at school or anywhere else again.

"Do you want to stop and pick some flowers?" Mark called back to Mattie as they rode their bikes home from school that afternoon. Once again, Calvin was up ahead.

"Not today," Mattie shouted. "I just want to go home and head straight to my room."

Mark slowed his bicycle and waited for Mattie to catch up with him. As she came alongside, he said, "Don't think I want to get any of those sparkly rocks today, either. I'm not lookin' forward to going home and telling Mom and Dad that I missed a bunch of words on the spelling test."

"I don't want to tell Mom about my slip falling off 'cause I was trying to do one hundred jumps, either." Mattie frowned. "She'll probably say I deserved it for being full of hochmut."

"I'll bet Mom will say that to me, too," Mark said. "But I think it's all right to brag a little when you know you're really good at something, don't you?"

"Maybe," Mattie said. "Only thing is, neither of us is as good as we thought. If we were, then you wouldn't have missed any spelling words, and I would've made one hundred jumps without anything bad happening to me. Well, at least no one laughed when I walked back into class. Guess that's something to be grateful for."

"You can thank Karen Yoder for that," Mark said. "She warned everyone not to tease you, plus Calvin and I both said something, too."

"Danki for that, Mark. It'll make going to school tomorrow a little easier."

"One thing for sure," Mark said as he pedaled harder again, "I'm glad Friday is our last day of school. I can't wait to start having some summer fun."

"Me, too," Mattie agreed. "One of the things I'd like to teach Twinkles is to bark when she needs to go outside. Oh, and before I start having any summer fun, I have some baking to do, 'cause this Friday for the school picnic I'll be taking a yummy cake I'm gonna bake."

Mark smacked his lips. "Yum. I can hardly wait for that. Maybe you can practice by making a cake for our family to eat one night this week. That way you'll know if it's good enough to take to school on Friday as a treat."

"That's a good idea," Mattie agreed. She started pedaling harder and zipped right past Mark.

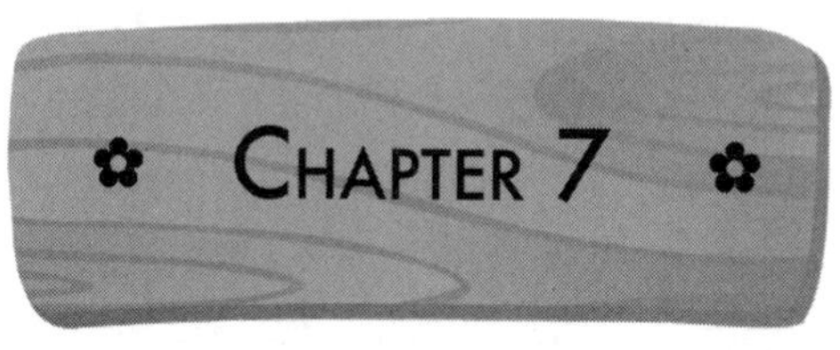

Last Day of School

It took Mattie the rest of the week to get over what had happened to her at school, even if her classmates had obviously forgotten about it. Of course, Mark had an equally bad day because of his poor grade on his spelling test. Fortunately for Calvin, he'd gotten a perfect score on his test, but he hadn't bragged about it. At least one part of Mattie's day had gone well, since she'd also gotten a perfect score, and she guessed that was really more important than being upset because her slip had fallen off. And she had learned a good lesson about bragging.

Mom had been sympathetic to both of the twins, but she'd reminded Mattie and Mark about the dangers of boasting. She'd also fixed Mattie's slip so it would stay in place. Dad had agreed with Mom about bragging, and to help the twins understand a little better, he'd quoted Psalm 25:9 during supper Tuesday night: "He guides the humble in what is right and teaches them his way."

Friday morning as Mattie put her cake in the box Mom and Dad would take to the schoolhouse later on, she felt more content. It was a German raw apple cake, and she'd made it last night all by herself.

Mattie smiled as she gazed at the yummy-looking cake. She was sure it would be the best-tasting dessert at the school picnic today, but she would try not to be prideful or brag about it. Mattie was also excited about the baseball game they'd play after their meal, with many of the parents and children taking part in the game. Since she was such a good ballplayer, she was sure her team would win.

"Are you ready to go now, Mattie?" Mark asked, moving toward the door. "Calvin left five minutes ago."

She nodded and gave Mom a hug good-bye. "Don't forget to bring my cake when you come to the schoolhouse for the program today," she reminded.

"I won't forget," said Mom, giving Mattie's shoulder a squeeze.

"And you don't want to be late," Mark called over his shoulder. "I'll be saying my recitation, and I'd be disappointed if you missed it."

"We'll be on time," Mom assured the twins. "Now hurry along, or you'll be late for school."

"Think I'll stop on the way and pick some *blumme* for Anna Ruth," Mattie told Mark as they climbed on their bikes. "Since I don't have any money to buy a gift for our teacher, some pretty flowers would be nice."

"That may be true, but you don't have time for picking blumme," Mark said. "Remember what Mom told us about hurrying so we won't be late?"

Mattie sighed. "It won't take me long, and I'm not gonna be late." She pedaled up the driveway and out of the yard, leaving Mark to follow.

A short time later, Mattie spotted some pretty wildflowers growing near the edge of the path, so she stopped pedaling and got off the bike. "See you at school," she called to Mark as he rode on by.

Knowing she didn't have long to pick, Mattie quickly gathered up a nice bouquet. Then she placed them in the plastic bag she'd brought along, put it in her basket, and headed for school. When she got there, the bell hadn't rung yet, because many of her schoolmates were out in the yard. That was a relief!

Mattie had just started talking to Stella, when a drop of rain splattered her nose. Then more drops came, and soon it was pouring. Mattie, along with the rest of the scholars, raced into the schoolhouse, even though their teacher hadn't rung the bell.

"Sure hope the rain stops before our parents get here," Mattie said to her friend.

"I hope so, too," Stella replied. "Bad weather could ruin our picnic, and we might not get to play baseball."

Mattie's shoulders slumped, and her mouth turned down at the corners. She hoped the rain would stop by then, because she wanted to show everyone in her family how well she could play.

As the scholars awaited their family and friends' arrival, Mark's heart started to pound. What if he forgot his recitation? After messing up on the spelling test earlier this week, he needed to do well today.

Mark glanced out the window. It was still raining. If it kept on, they would eat their meal in the schoolhouse basement, but it would also mean there'd be no baseball game. *That'd be fine with me,* Mark thought. *Then I won't be expected to play.*

He looked at Mattie and noticed her gaze was focused on the rain, too. Since his twin was such a good ballplayer, she was probably hoping the weather would improve.

Mark tried to listen to Anna Ruth, but it was hard to concentrate on the teacher as she went over the activities that would be taking place once the parents arrived. All Mark could do was repeat the lines from his recitation over and over in his head. For some reason, he'd felt better at home when he had practiced memorizing his part. But this was different. He'd be reciting with three other students. With all eyes on them, what if the others did well, but he flubbed up his lines? He didn't want to embarrass himself in front of his family and the other parents, not to mention his classmates.

The *clippety-clop-clop* of horses' hooves drove Mark's thoughts aside. The parents were beginning to arrive. Now Mark really felt nervous.

Mark's stomach twisted as he took his place at the front of the room, along with the three other students, ready to say their recitations. Mark's friend John was the first to say his lines, and he did well. Then Sharon and Mary recited their parts, and everything went fine for them, too.

With sweaty palms, Mark drew in a deep breath and thought, *Here goes nothing*. He started out by holding up a piece of white cardboard with a picture of a bee painted on it. "Some people are afraid of bees because they can sting, but there's a type of bee that is good for making honey," he said. "The word *bee* can help us remember many things: Be helpful. Be courteous. Be generous. Be grateful. Be appreciative. Be humble."

When Mark finished, he felt pleased. He'd said all of his lines perfectly, without a single mistake. Mom, Dad, Grandpa and Grandma Miller, as well as his brothers and sisters were all smiling at him. He was proud of himself and held his head high. Now if the rain would just continue so they didn't have to play ball, it would be a perfect day.

Mattie couldn't believe it was still raining, but it had continued throughout the program. Now it was time for lunch, and everyone headed to the basement, where all the food had been put on tables. More tables and backless wooden benches would be used for people to sit while they ate.

Mattie knew there couldn't be a ball game in this weather, which was a big disappointment. But she still had her delicious German raw apple cake to look forward to. Other desserts had been brought today, too, along with hot dishes, salads, pickles, chips, bread, and butter.

After everyone said a silent prayer, they helped themselves to the food. Mattie was tempted to walk over to the dessert table and take a piece of her cake right away, but she knew Mom would tell her to eat something else before going after the desserts. Mattie's eyes were drawn to the center of the food table. It delighted her to see that Anna Ruth had used the flowers she'd given her for a centerpiece. They added more festive color with everything else on the table.

"See those flowers?" Mattie said to her friend Stella, as they stood in line to dish up their food. "I picked them for our teacher this morning. And see that cake over there on the dessert table? I made it myself, so be sure to try a piece."

"The bouquet is pretty, and your cake looks good, too. What kind is it?" Stella asked, while looking at the dessert Mattie had pointed to.

"It's a German raw apple cake, and it's one of my favorite kinds. I got the recipe from Grandma Troyer."

Stella smiled. "Oh, that's right, she's your mamm's

mother, and she and your grandpa Troyer live up in Geauga County."

Mattie nodded. "I wish they could be here today, too, but at least my *daed*'s folks, Grandma and Grandpa Miller, made it to the school program."

"My dad's parents live in Middlebury, Indiana, and my mom's folks live in Bird-in-Hand, Pennsylvania, so I don't have any grandparents here at all," Stella said with a downcast expression.

Mattie felt bad for her friend. She couldn't imagine not having any grandparents living nearby. It was nice to be able to stop by Grandpa and Grandma Miller's house as often as she wanted. Grandpa always had funny stories to tell, and he usually had a piece of gum for Mattie and her siblings. Grandma was just as special. She never let Mattie or any of her brothers or little sister leave without giving them cookies or some other special treat that she'd baked in her oven.

"You're welcome to go with me sometime when I visit Grandma Miller," Mattie said. "Grandma has lots of beautiful blumme in her yard this time of the year, and I'll bet she'd let us pick some. And if we don't make it there this summer, maybe we can go in the fall, because there will be plenty of flowers then, too."

"That would be fun," Stella said as she put some chicken-rice casserole on her plate.

After Mattie had chosen all the food she wanted, she headed across the room to take a seat with the rest of her family. As they ate and visited with others, all Mattie could think about was her cake sitting on the dessert table. She hoped it didn't get eaten up before everyone in her family got a taste.

"Mark, you did a good job on your recitation during the play," Grandpa Miller said. He chuckled and gave his long gray beard a quick tug. "I half expected you to use some big word that no one would understand. You know, maybe something like *deviate* or *astronomical*."

"I know that *deviate* means 'to turn aside or differ,'" Mattie spoke up, "because I've heard Mark use that word. But what does *astronomical* mean?"

"It means 'extremely large or enormous,'" Mark replied with a crooked grin.

There he goes, showing off again, Mattie thought. *I'll bet he does that so people will think he's schmaert. Well, wait till they've had a taste of the cake I made. Then they'll think I'm pretty smart, too.*

After everyone had finished eating, the pies, cakes, and cookies were taken out of their containers. Since Mattie wanted her family to eat some of the cake she'd made, she hurried across the room, picked up the cake, and started back to their table. She was halfway there when her little sister, Ada, darted across the room and bumped into Mattie. Mattie's hand slipped, and the cake fell on the floor.

"Ach, no!" Mattie cried, going down on her knees. "My cake is ruined, and now no one will be able to taste it!"

Chapter 8

The Flu Bug

When Mattie woke up the following morning, she rolled over and listened for the sound of droplets falling off the roof and pelting the ground. She noticed right away that it had quit raining, because there wasn't a sound.

Mattie groaned and stretched her arms over her head. *Why couldn't it have been nice like this yesterday so we could've played baseball?* she wondered. To make matters worse, since she'd dropped her cake, no one had been able to taste it. Mom had given Mattie sympathy and helped her clean up the mess, and Grandma Miller said she hoped Mattie would make the cake again so she could taste it. Even so, Mattie felt bad and wished the last day of school had gone better.

Well, school was finally over, and today was a new day. Hopefully, Mom wouldn't expect her to do a bunch of chores like she did some Saturdays, because Mattie had other plans. She wanted to spend some time working with Twinkles in order to teach her how to bark when she needed to go out. She was also hoping to lie in the new hammock Dad had found at a yard sale a few weeks ago. It would be a good place to daydream or take a nap, or even to lie there and quietly watch for the baby bunny she'd seen a few days ago.

Maybe I'll pick some of my flowers that are blooming right now, she thought as she climbed out of bed. *It would be nice to bring some inside and put them in a vase.*

Mattie hurried to get dressed and then went down the hall to the bathroom to wash up before heading to the kitchen to set the table for breakfast. The funny thing was, she didn't hear any sounds coming from the kitchen—no humming that Mom usually did or any clattering of dishes. There was no coffee aroma or any other smells, either, which seemed strange.

When Mattie went downstairs, she was surprised that Mom wasn't in the kitchen. A few minutes later, Ada came in, rubbing her eyes. "Where's Mom?" she asked, looking around the room.

"I don't know," Mattie replied. "I thought she'd be here, making breakfast."

"I'm hungerich." Ada rubbed her tummy.

"Jah, me too." Mattie helped Ada sit on her stool. Then she poured her a glass of apple juice. "You can drink this while I go see if I can find Mom."

Ada lifted the glass to her lips and took a drink. "*Is gut*," she said, smacking her lips.

"Jah, apple juice is always good." Mattie smiled and hurried down the hall toward Mom and Dad's bedroom.

The door was shut, and she was about to knock, when Dad stepped out. "Be real quiet," he said, putting his finger to his lips. "Your mamm is sleeping."

"How come?" Mattie questioned. "I thought she'd have breakfast ready by now."

"Said she feels achy and nauseous, and her forehead's hot, so she's obviously *grank*," Dad said. "I told her to stay in bed."

Mattie felt concern hearing that Mom was sick. "Sure hope it's nothing serious."

Dad shook his head. "It's probably the flu. I heard it's been going around lately, and with so many people at the school program yesterday, she could have easily caught the bug."

"Mom caught a bug?" Perry asked, padding down the hall toward them with a curious expression. "Was it a fly or a spider?"

Dad and Mattie chuckled. "No," Dad said, more seriously. "Your mamm is sick in bed, and I think she caught the flu bug."

Perry scrunched up his face. "Who's gonna fix breakfast this mornin' if Mom's grank?"

"Mattie, I'm hungerich!" Ada called from the kitchen.

Dad gave Perry's shoulder a tap. "I'm sure Mattie can fix you and your little sister something to eat. Now hurry off to the kitchen, and don't bother your mamm today. She needs her rest."

Mattie glanced at her parents' bedroom door then

up at Dad. "If Mom will be in bed all day, who's gonna watch Ada and Perry?"

Dad smiled at Mattie. "I was hoping I could count on you for that."

"Can't you or one of my brieder look after them, Dad?" she asked.

He shook his head. "Ike, Russell, and I will be working in my shop most of the day. Calvin will be helping us for part of the day, too. I'll ask Mark to help you take care of Perry and Ada." Dad started down the hall toward the kitchen, and Mattie followed.

She frowned, thinking this wasn't a good way to start their summer vacation. With Mom being sick, Mattie would most likely have more chores to do. She wasn't happy, either, about having to watch her little brother and sister, but at least Mark would be there to help out.

"I'm sorry to hear Mom is sick in bed," Ike said as the family sat around the kitchen table, eating the cereal Mattie had set out for their breakfast.

Dad nodded. "I don't want any of you to catch the flu, so you'd best stay away from your mamm until she's well." He looked at Mark. "I expect you to help Mattie with Perry and Ada, because Mattie will also be busy getting our meals ready today."

"Someone needs to check on Mom and take her some food," Mattie commented. "I'll get a dish from the cupboard and pour her a bowl of cereal."

Dad took a drink of coffee. "She has no appetite, but I made sure she has plenty of water. What your mamm needs more than anything right now is no interruptions and lots of rest."

"Bet I wouldn't get the flu if I got around Mom," Mark boasted. "I'm healthy and strong and hardly ever get sick."

"The flu bug can hit anyone," Ike cautioned. "So you'd better do as Dad said and stay out of Mom's room."

Mark didn't think he should argue with his big brother, so he just shrugged his shoulders and drank down the rest of his milk. He wouldn't go into Mom's room unless he needed to ask her something important.

After everyone finished breakfast, Dad and the older boys went out to the shop, while Mattie cleared the dishes. "Can you keep an eye on Perry and Ada and help 'em find something to do?" she asked Mark.

Mark frowned. "Why can't you do that, Mattie?"

She motioned to the sink. "I have dishes to wash. 'Course, if you'd rather do the dishes, I'd be happy to take our little brother and sister outside to play."

Mark shook his head vigorously. "No way! I'll take 'em outside. Just don't be long, okay? I have other things I'd like to do today that don't include Ada and Perry."

"Like what?" Mattie questioned.

"For one thing, I'm planning to practice playing basketball." Mark grinned. "I'm glad Grandpa was able to put a new net on the hoop Thursday afternoon, and then Ike got it put up on the barn right away. And I'm thankful Calvin and Russell bought a basketball so we can all play."

Mattie frowned. "It wouldn't be fair if I have to watch Ada and Perry all day and you get to play."

"I'll be keeping an eye on them while you do the dishes, remember?"

"Jah, but that's only for a short time. It won't take me that long to wash and dry the dishes. In case you've forgotten, Dad asked you to help take care of Ada and Perry," she quickly added.

"Okay, I know, but let's not talk about this anymore, Mattie. We're just wastin' time." Mark turned to Perry and Ada and said, "Kumme now. Let's go outside."

Wearing big smiles, they both got down from their stools and followed him out the door. Once outside, Mark got them busy playing a game of tag. They'd only been playing a short while, when Mark's friend John came riding in on his bike.

"What are you up to?" John called after he'd parked the bike near their barn.

"Just playing a game with Perry and Ada while Mattie does the dishes," Mark replied. "Mom's grank, so she'll be in bed all day."

"Sorry to hear that. Has she got the flu?" John asked. "Heard it's been goin' around lately."

Mark nodded.

"Came by to see if you'd like to go fishin' with me," John said. "But if ya have to watch your sister and brother today, then I guess ya can't go."

"Oh, I don't have to watch them all day," Mark was quick to say. "Just till Mattie's done with the dishes. She'll take over after that."

John smiled. "Can we go fishing then?"

"Don't see why not. 'Course, I'll have to check with Mom about it first."

John's brows furrowed. "But if she's grank then you probably don't want to go in her room."

Mark flapped his hand. "I'm not worried about that. I hardly ever get sick."

"That's good," John said. "I had the flu a few years ago, and it was awful. My muscles were so sore that it felt like a horse and buggy had run over me."

"I heard it can be pretty bad." Mark slowly shook his head, wishing Mom wasn't sick.

"Say, did ya ever get your basketball hoop cleaned up and painted?" John asked.

"Sure did. It's hanging on the other side of our barn, all fixed up, good as new. I'll have to show you later, when Mattie comes out of the house and takes over watching Ada and Perry."

John looked toward the barn where Mark was pointing. "Wow, I can't wait to see it. Did ya find a net for it, too?"

"Jah. Grandpa Miller had an old fishing net he

wasn't using, and it worked perfectly for the netting on the hoop."

Mark and John walked toward the house, talking more about basketball, as Mark's two cats zipped past them and onto the porch.

"Sure will be fun playing basketball with you this summer," John said.

Mark nodded. This was going to be a fun summer: playing basketball, going fishing, and whatever else came along. The summer months lay ahead, and they had a good many weeks to enjoy them.

"You know, even after summer is over, we still might have something to look forward to. If it works out, that is," Mark added. "I was thinking we could ask our daeds about taking us camping in the fall instead of summer. The autumn months are cooler, and it will be fun to sit around the campfire at night. What do you think about that, John?"

"Sounds like a good idea," John replied with enthusiasm. "But let's enjoy our summer first."

Mark gestured to Perry and Ada, who'd taken seats on the porch and were petting Mark's cats. "If you'll keep an eye on them while I'm gone, I'll go ask Mom if I can go fishing with you."

John nodded. "Jah, sure, I can do that." He flopped down on the porch beside Perry and started petting Boots. Mark knew John liked cats, because he'd given him one of Lucky's kittens last year, and John took good care of the cat he'd named Tippy.

"I'll be right back," Mark said. He raced into the house to talk to Mom.

Change of Plans

Tap! Tap! Tap! Mark rapped on his mother's bedroom door.

"Who is it?" Mom called in a weak voice.

"It's me, Mark."

"I'm grank, so you'd better not come in."

Mark opened the door a crack and peered into the darkened room. Mom was lying in bed with a washcloth on her forehead. "It's okay, Mom; I'm not worried about getting sick." Mark stepped into the room and moved slowly toward the bed. He watched as Mom squeezed her eyes shut. "I need to ask you a question."

"Okay, but first, could you close the door a little more? The light coming into the room is hurting my eyes," she said, holding one hand over her eyes.

"Sorry, Mom. I didn't think about that," Mark apologized and hurriedly pushed the door closed so that no light from the hall would get into the room.

"Don't come too close," Mom warned when Mark moved closer to the bed. "I've been sick to my stomach and can't keep any food down. Now, what's your question?" she asked, opening her eyes a little.

"Is it all right if I go fishing with John?"

"I suppose it would be okay—unless your daed asked you to do something for him today."

Mark shook his head. "The only thing Dad asked me to do was help Mattie with Ada and Perry."

"Who's watching them now?" Mom questioned.

"Mattie will be doing that as soon as she's done with the breakfast dishes," Mark replied. "But my friend John is on the porch with Ada and Perry, till I go back outside."

"Does Mattie care if you run off with John?"

Mark shrugged. "Don't think she'd have a problem with it." In his heart, he knew his twin probably wouldn't like the idea, but maybe he could convince her that she could manage without him for a while.

Mom sighed, closing her eyes again. "If Mattie's okay with it, then you have my permission to go fishing."

Mark reached out and touched his mother's hand. He could see from her pale face and flushed cheeks that she wasn't feeling well. "Danki, Mom. I hope you feel better soon."

"I hope so, too, because I have a household to run," Mom said, without opening her eyes.

As Mark tiptoed out of the room and quietly closed the door, he said a silent prayer. *Dear God, please help my mamm to get well quickly. I feel bad that she's grank.*

✿

When Mattie finished putting the last dish away, she went outside to see how Mark was doing with Ada and Perry. What she discovered was her little brother and sister sitting on the porch with Mark's friend John. There was no sign of Mark.

"Where's my twin brother?" Mattie asked.

"He went to the barn to get his fishing pole," John replied with a smile.

Mattie blinked rapidly. "Fishing pole? What does Mark need that for? He said he was going to play basketball today."

John shrugged. "Guess he changed his mind when I came over and invited him to go fishin' with me."

She shook her head. "Mark can't go fishing. He has to stay here and help me take care of Ada and Perry 'cause our mamm is grank."

"I heard she was. Hope she feels better soon."

"Me too."

Just then Mark showed up, carrying his fishing pole. "Hey, Mattie, did you get the dishes done?" he asked.

She nodded quickly. "I hear you're planning to go fishing with John."

"Jah, Mom said I could go."

"Why did you go to see Mom?" Mattie questioned. "Didn't you hear what Dad said about that?"

"Jah, but I'm sure I'll be fine. Like I said earlier, I

hardly ever get sick."

"Well, you also said you would help me look after Ada and Perry. I don't think Dad would like you running off and leaving me to take care of them by myself while you go fishing. That wouldn't be fair."

"Said I'd watch 'em while you washed and dried the dishes." Mark acted like he didn't even care about helping, and Mattie's irritation grew when her brother turned to John and said, "Should we get going now?"

Before John could reply, Mattie stepped between them. "You weren't watching Ada and Perry at all. John was. But that's beside the point. Please don't go fishing, Mark. I think you oughta stay close in case I need help with our little sister and brother today. And what if Mom needs us for something?" she added.

"I think Mattie's right," John chimed in. "We can stay here and find something fun to do and go fishing some other time. We have the whole summer to enjoy that. This way you'll be close by if you're needed."

"Oh, okay," Mark finally agreed. "So, how about a game of basketball? We can try out my new hoop."

John grinned, bobbing his head. "That sounds like fun, and you did promise to show me the hoop you found."

"Can I play, too?" Perry asked, leaving his seat on the porch.

"You're too little," Mark said. "You'd never be able to throw the ball high enough to make a basket."

Perry thrust out his bottom lip. "It ain't fair. I never

get to do anything fun."

"That's not true." Mattie was tempted to correct his English but decided to let it go, since Perry was upset. "You had fun playing tag with me and Ada," she reminded her little brother.

"I guess so, but I'd rather play ball with John and Mark."

John put his hand on Perry's shoulder. "Why don't you come along and watch us play? Maybe you can keep score for us."

Perry's eyes brightened as he bounced on his toes. "Okay!"

Mattie breathed a sigh of relief. Since Perry would be with Mark, all she had to worry about was keeping Ada entertained.

When the boys headed to the other side of the barn where the hoop hung, Mattie called for Ada to follow her into the house. They'd no more than stepped into the kitchen when Dad showed up. "How are things going, Mattie?" he asked.

"Okay, I guess. Mark's friend John is here, and they're out playing basketball. Oh, and Perry's with them. They said he could keep score."

Dad chuckled. "Well, he's a pretty schmaert boy, so maybe he can."

"Did you need something?" Mattie asked. "I could make some sandwiches if you or the brothers are getting hungerich yet."

He shook his head. "It's too early for lunch. I just came in from the shop to check on your mamm. I want to see how she's feeling and make sure she has enough water to drink."

"Mark went in to see Mom awhile ago," Mattie said. Realizing that it sounded like she was tattling, she wished she could take back her words. But it was too late for that now.

Dad's thick eyebrows furrowed. "He went in after I told everyone at breakfast not to disturb your mamm? I'll need to talk with him about that."

"Mark wanted to ask her a question and said he didn't think he would get sick."

"There's a possibility that any of us could get the flu, even without going close to your mamm," Dad said. "But it will lessen your chances if you stay away from our room and let me tend to your mamm."

"But you might get grank if you get too close to Mom," Mattie mentioned.

"You're right, and that's why I'm being careful to wash my hands regularly." Dad went to the sink and filled a glass with water; then he placed a few soda crackers on a small plate. "I'm taking these in to your mamm now, and I'll be back to check on her several times throughout the day. In the meantime, if she needs anything, I'll tell her to call out to you, and then you can come out to the shop and get me. Okay?"

Mattie nodded. She hoped Mom got better soon.

Dad was concerned, too, for she could see the worry lines on his bearded face.

Well, she thought, sighing deeply, *it's too soon for lunch, but I guess I could at least try to figure out what to fix when the time comes to make it. Maybe I'll make some cheese sandwiches, since that'd be easy. For dessert, we can have some of those peanut butter cookies Mom made the other day.*

"Wow, you're really good at this game! You must have been practicing a lot," John said after Mark shot his fifth basket in a row. Already Perry had given up counting and was kneeling on the grass, petting both of Mark's cats.

"Not really." Mark shook his head. "I think since I've grown taller now, it helps, not to mention that I have a good aim."

"I'm as tall as you, and I've missed most of my shots." John frowned. "Guess maybe I need more practice."

The boys continued to play, with Mark still making more baskets than his friend. Finally, the game came to a halt when Perry complained that he was hungry.

"Why don't we all go into the house and see about having a snack?" Mark suggested.

Perry jumped up and clapped his hands. "That's a good idea, Mark!"

"All right, let's go." Mark put the ball aside, and the

three boys hurried to the house. When they entered the kitchen, Mark saw Mattie and Ada sitting at the table, eating cookies and milk.

"We came in for a snack," he said, pulling out a chair and taking a seat. Before Mattie could comment, Mark snatched a cookie off the plate and took a big bite. "Umm. . .this is appenditlich."

"You should wash your hands before you eat," Mattie scolded. "That goes for you, too, Perry and John."

Mark pushed away from the table. "Guess you're right about that." He went to the kitchen sink and washed his hands. Perry and John did the same, only Perry had to use a stool in order to reach the sink. When they were done, they returned to the table and Mattie gave them each three cookies and a glass of milk.

"This should hold us all till lunch. Oh, and when you're finished eating, are you going back outside?" Mattie asked.

"Maybe," Mark replied. "Why do you ask?"

"Just wondered if you could watch Ada for a while. I want to go outside and pick some blumme to cheer Mom up. If I take Ada along, she'll only get in the way."

Mark groaned. "I suppose I could watch her, but only for a little while. John and I want to shoot some more hoops."

"It won't take me much time at all," Mattie said. "In fact, I'll go right now." She took a pair of scissors from one of the kitchen drawers, grabbed a wicker basket, and headed out the door.

The next morning, Mark woke up with a headache. The rest of his body ached, too, and he felt sick to his stomach. “Oh, great,” he moaned. “Now both Mom and I are sick in bed.”

Mark couldn’t believe he’d come down with the flu. *Maybe I shouldn’t have bragged about hardly ever getting sick,* he thought with regret. *I probably caught the bug because I went into Mom’s room.* Then he remembered that not only had he touched Mom’s hand, but he’d also eaten a cookie without washing his hands. He’d been hoping to ride his bike later this afternoon to get those rocks he’d seen last week. *Guess I should have done that on my way home from school on Friday, but it was raining and I didn’t want to stop. Now I can’t go anywhere ’cause I feel so lousy. I’m so dumm for getting close to Mom while she has the flu, and even dumber for not washing my hands.*

Tap! Tap! Tap! “Breakfast is ready, Mark,” Mattie called through the closed door.

Mark groaned. Just the thought of food made his stomach roll, and the smell of cooked bacon coming from the kitchen just made things worse. “I’m sick, Mattie. Think I caught the flu from Mom.”

“Oh, great. I’m sorry to hear that, but I’m not surprised since you went into Mom’s room when you were told not to," Mattie said.

Mark made no comment. Mattie was right, but he felt too sick to talk about it.

"I'll let Dad know. I'm sure he'll be in to check on you."

Pulling the covers up to his chin, Mark wondered if anyone else in the family might get sick. He closed his eyes and prayed, *Dear Lord, please keep everyone well, and help me and Mom to get better soon, 'cause it's no fun being grank, especially now with school being out.*

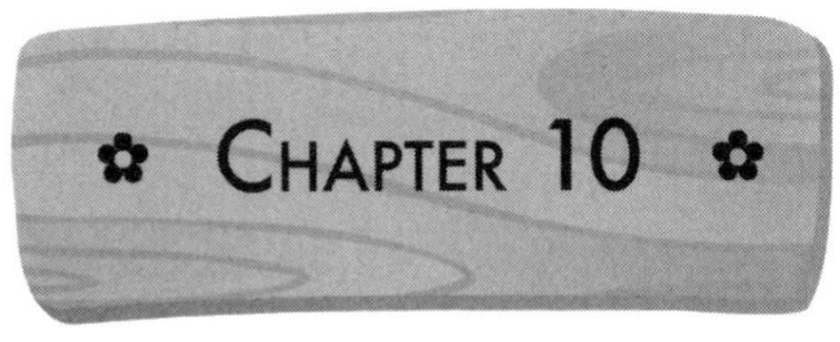

Trouble with Twinkles

The days seemed to fly by, and it was already the first week of June. Mark had gone to the pond near their home with John that morning, but so far they hadn't done any fishing. The sun felt so good as it beat down on Mark's head, and it almost put him to sleep. *Too bad every day can't be as nice as this one,* he thought, leaning back on his elbows and looking up at the cloudless, sunny sky.

"Sure hope I catch a lot of fish today," Mark said, glancing over at John. "Both sets of our grandparents will be at our place this evening, and Mom said if I catch a bunch of fish she'll cook 'em for supper. If I get some nice big fat ones, I'll bet Grandpa Miller will be proud of me, 'cause he's real good at fishing."

John smiled. "Think my mamm would like to have some fish to fry for supper tonight, too."

The boys sat quietly for a while. Then Mark said, "Sure is nice to be here at the pond, but if we don't get busy neither of us will catch any fish."

"You're right about that," John agreed. "Can't sit here all day, soakin' up the sun and watchin' the clouds roll by while we talk about the fish we'd like to catch."

Mark snickered. "Guess we'd better get busy then."

The boys baited their hooks and cast their lines into the water. As Mark waited for a fish to bite, he thought about the time he and Mattie had gone fishing with Grandpa Miller and how Mattie had caught the most fish. Mark hadn't liked that at all, and he'd been envious of her.

Today wouldn't be like that, though, because Mattie wasn't here. Of course, there was always the chance that John would catch more fish than him. If that happened, Mark wouldn't have anything to boast about.

Thinking about bragging caused Mark to remember how he had boasted about rarely getting sick, but then he'd come down with the flu. At least he hadn't had a relapse, the way Mom had when she'd gotten out of bed too soon. It had taken her almost a week to feel better, which meant Mark and Mattie had been given a lot more responsibilities. When the twins complained about all the work, Dad said it wouldn't hurt them to do extra chores or keep an eye on their little brother and sister. He told them that working helped to build character and was a lesson in learning about responsibility.

Mark supposed Dad was right, even though he'd rather play than work. He also knew that he had to do what his dad said. Besides, when he'd seen how much Mom appreciated all the help, Mark felt a bit proud of himself for doing such a good job helping with things.

"Here, Twinkles!" Mattie called as she stood on the porch with her hands cupped around her mouth. Grandpa and Grandma Troyer were coming to spend a few days, and they would arrive sometime this afternoon. This evening, Grandma and Grandma Miller would be joining all of them for supper, so Mattie wanted Twinkles to be clean and smelling nice. She'd also baked another German raw apple cake, which she planned to serve for dessert. Mattie was sure her cake would be a hit, and already she felt quite proud. Tonight, she would be extra careful when she carried it to the table.

"Whatcha doin' out here on the porch?" Perry asked when he came outside. "Thought you was gonna give Twinkles a bath."

"The word is *were* not *was*," Mattie corrected. "And I am planning to bathe my dog just as soon as I find her."

"Need some help givin' Twinkles her bath?" her little brother asked with a hopeful expression.

She shook her head. "Danki anyway, but I'm sure I can manage." Truth was, Mattie thought Perry would just get in the way, and they'd probably end up with more water on him than the dog. Sometimes when

Perry or Ada was around, Twinkles got all excited and wouldn't behave. That was one of the reasons she occasionally had an accident in the house. So Mattie thought it would be better if she bathed the dog herself.

Perry gave Mattie's arm a little shake. "Want me to help ya find your hund?"

Mattie smiled and nodded. "Jah, sure, that'd be great." After all, if two people looked for Twinkles, they'd probably find her sooner. Then Mattie could get the dog's bath over quickly and have time to do something else before Grandma and Grandpa Troyer arrived. Besides, it would make Perry feel like he was helping, and he wouldn't be in the way, searching for the dog.

"Why don't I go look in the barn, and you can search all around the yard?" Mattie suggested. "If you find her, yell real loud so I can hear you. Okay?"

Perry nodded then darted around to the front of the house.

Mattie hurried to the barn. Inside, Mark's two cats, meowing and swishing their tails, ran up to greet her. "Go away, you two," Mattie said, sidestepping the cats. "I don't have time to pet you right now."

Boots followed Mattie and rubbed against her legs. *P-r-r-r-r. P-r-r-r-r.* Her little black head bobbed as her throat softly vibrated. Soon, Lucky joined them, also purring and pushing against Mattie's legs, wanting her attention.

Mattie didn't wish to be mean to the cats, but she

didn't have time for this right now. So she took the bag of cat food down from the nearby shelf and poured some into Boots's and Lucky's dishes. That did the trick, for they both forgot about being petted and darted over to their dishes, where they began crunching the food.

Mattie headed to the other side of the barn, calling for Twinkles. There was no sign of the dog. Not even a whimper. *Could she be hiding?* Mattie wondered. *Does she sense that I'm planning to give her a bath?* Twinkles didn't seem to mind plodding through mud puddles or running back and forth through the sprinkler, but she didn't cooperate whenever it was time for a bath. Mattie wondered if her dog preferred to be dirty and smelly, or could Twinkles be afraid of the deeper water in the tub? Well it didn't matter, because Mattie was determined to give her dog a bath today.

Mattie continued to search all around the barn, calling, "Here, Twinkles! Come here, girl." Then an idea popped into her head. Since the cats had gone straight to their dishes when she'd poured them some food, maybe that would work for Twinkles, too.

Mattie went to another shelf where the dog's food was kept, took down the bag, and shook it. Then she poured some into Twinkles's dish. Mattie stood back, folded her arms, and waited. She swiped at an annoying fly that kept buzzing around her head. Several minutes went by, but there was no sign of Twinkles. Hoping her dog would hear the shaking of the dog food bag, or at least hear it pouring loudly into the bowl, Mattie soon realized that neither of those things had worked. She'd finally been able to teach her dog to bark when she was in the house and needed to go out, but now she couldn't even get her to come to her when she called.

Mattie was about to call the dog's name again, when Perry shouted from outside, "I found her, Mattie!"

Mattie stepped out of the barn, but she didn't see Twinkles or Perry anywhere. "Where are you, Perry, and where's my hund?" she hollered, looking around the yard.

"We're over here," Perry called.

Mattie glanced toward Dad's market buggy, parked outside his woodshop. Then she spotted Twinkles with her furry little head sticking out the opening of the passenger's side. Perry was also in the buggy, sitting in the driver's seat.

Mattie hurried across the yard and over to the buggy. "What are you two doing in there?"

"I think Twinkles was in the buggy the whole time," Perry explained. "Since the side door was open, guess she must've jumped in." He grinned at Mattie, looking rather pleased with himself. "I got in with her to make sure she didn't jump out and run away. Aren't ya glad I found her?"

"Jah, I sure am. Danki, Perry." Mattie reached inside and scooped Twinkles into her arms. "Now you're coming with me, 'cause like or not, it's time for your bath. Come on, Perry. You should get out of the buggy now, too."

Woof! Twinkles tried to wiggle free.

"Oh no you don't," Mattie scolded. Walking toward the house, she looked back and was glad to see that Perry had climbed out of the buggy like she'd asked him to do.

When Mattie entered the house a few minutes later, she headed straight for the bathroom and quickly shut the door. She knew if she didn't, Twinkles would run off and hide. She didn't know why the dog disliked taking a bath so much, for Mattie found soaking in the bathtub with lots of bubbles to be very relaxing. But ever since she'd given Twinkles her first bath when she was a pup, the dog had tried to get out of the tub.

"You're getting a bath today, and that's all there is to it," Mattie mumbled as she filled the bathtub with enough warm water to bathe the dog. When that was done, she picked up Twinkles, who'd been cowering in the corner of the bathroom near the sink, and held her over the tub so that just her four paws touched the water. She hoped this might give the dog a chance to adjust to the idea of getting wet before putting her in.

Mattie giggled when Twinkles began paddling with her feet, as though she were swimming. She held the dog like that for a few seconds and then slowly lowered her into the water.

Twinkles whimpered and let out a *yip*, as if something terrible had just happened to her.

"Calm down, girl. You're okay," Mattie said, wetting Twinkles's coat thoroughly and then pouring some shampoo over the dog's dirty hair. Then she rubbed Twinkles's body all over with a wet cloth, making sure she was good and clean.

Next, using a plastic pitcher, Mattie poured clean water on Twinkles to remove the soap. Twinkles didn't like that much and started flipping her head back and forth, splattering water in Mattie's face.

"Absatz!" Mattie hollered. "Just hold still till I'm done." She poured more water over the dog.

Yip! Yip! Yip! Just as Mattie pulled the plug to let the bathwater out of the tub, Twinkles shook her whole body, sending a spray of water all over the place.

Mattie grimaced. Her dress, apron, and even her head covering were sopping wet, not to mention the floor, where more water had sprayed.

Quickly, Mattie lifted Twinkles out of the tub and wrapped a towel around her shivering wet body. It was hard to manage all of this, as she held on to the dog with one hand and grabbed another towel to wipe up the wet floor. The last thing she wanted was for someone to slip and hurt themselves when they came in to use the bathroom.

Once that was accomplished, Mattie started to dry her dog, who looked rather funny, dripping wet. Twinkles tried to get away, but Mattie held on tight and kept rubbing with the towel. Once the dog was dry enough, Mattie picked her up, but unexpectedly Perry opened the door. "How's it goin'?" he asked. "Need any help, or is Twinkles done with her bath?"

Arf! Arf! Twinkles wiggled out of Mattie's grip and darted out of the bathroom, zipping down the hall. Mattie raced after her, dripping water from her wet clothes onto the floor.

Just then, Mom opened the back door to shake out her dust mop, and Twinkles ran out. "Come back here!" Mattie shouted.

Twinkles kept running. Then she dropped to the ground and rolled on the grass.

Mattie clapped her hands and hollered, "Come here right now, Twinkles!" It seemed as though the pooch was trying to rub the clean smell off her little body.

Twinkles ignored Mattie and continued to roll all around. Then she jumped up and ran to find another spot to push herself through the green grass.

Disgusted, Mattie hurried to the spot where Twinkles lay, and was just getting ready to pick up Twinkles, when the dog leaped to her feet and raced out of the yard. Twinkles was sure full of energy. Either the bath had made her feel friskier than normal, or she wanted to rid herself of the clean smell as fast as she could.

Mattie groaned. *That was a wasted effort,* she thought. *By the time Twinkles comes home, she'll probably be dirty again, and there won't be enough time for me to give her another bath.*

“Guess Twinkles won’t be coming inside to see the grandparents when they get here,” Mattie muttered. Turning aside with a heavy sigh, she headed for her garden to pick some pretty flowers for their supper table.

While Mattie was busy selecting the flowers, Twinkles showed up and stood beside her as though watching. Bits of grass stuck to the dog’s coat, along with dirt in several places. The mutt didn’t smell very good, either—not like she would have if she hadn’t rolled around in the grass.

All of a sudden, Twinkles barked and looked toward Mattie’s garden sign. Mattie looked in the same direction and saw the cute little baby bunny huddling in the far corner. “Oh no you don’t, Twinkles.” Mattie caught hold of the dog before she had a chance to chase after the bunny.

“Twinkles, you’ve been nothing but trouble today,” Mattie scolded. She looked down at her dress and realized that she needed to change her clothes. Before she did that, however, she would brush the dirt and grass out of Twinkles’s hair to make her look better when their company arrived.

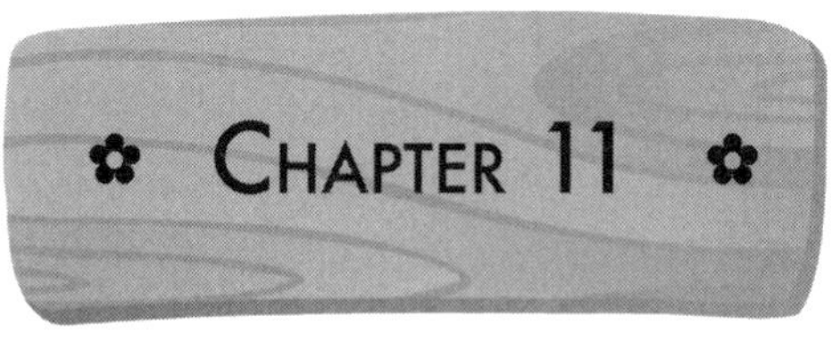

Good News

Mark whistled as he headed up the path toward home. He'd caught several nice fish today and was anxious to give them to Mom to fix for supper, even though he knew she also planned to serve baked chicken. Fishing with John had been a lot of fun, and Mark had ended up catching the biggest fish; although John caught two more than him. Mark thought the size of the fish was more important anyway, so he didn't care.

As Mark approached his house he spotted Grandpa Troyer sitting in the wicker rocking chair on the front porch. Twinkles sat next to Grandpa's chair, until she saw Mark coming up the walk. Then she leaped off the porch and ran up to him, wagging her tail. Before Mark knew what was happening, Twinkles jumped up and grabbed one of the fish, pulling it from the bucket Mark held. Before Mark could react, the naughty little dog took off across the yard.

"Come back here, Twinkles!" Mark shouted, chasing after the dog.

It took several trips around the yard, with Mark hollering for Twinkles to stop, before he finally caught her and took the fish back. With her tail between her legs, Twinkles slunk off to the barn.

Mark hurried his steps. When he joined Grandpa Troyer on the porch, he smiled and said, "Hi, Grandpa! I'm so glad you're here. Look at the fish I caught today."

Grandpa smiled, looking into the bucket Mark held. "Those are some nice ones, all right. It's a good thing you were able to get that one back from the dog before she ate it. You're pretty fast on your feet, my boy."

Mark grinned and bobbed his head. He hadn't always been able to run this fast, but since he'd grown taller, his legs seemed to move faster when he ran. "I'm gonna give the fish to Mom so she can fix 'em for supper tonight," he said.

Grandpa smacked his lips. "Bet they'll be real tasty, Mark."

"Where's Grandma?" Mark asked. "I want her to see my fish, too."

"She's in the kitchen with your mamm and Mattie. I'm sure she'll be happy to see you, as well as the fish you caught today."

Mark set the bucket on the porch and gave Grandpa a hug. "Sure am glad you and Grandma could come for a visit. We don't get to see you that often."

"I know," said Grandpa, nodding slowly. "We've been thinking about selling our place and moving down here to Holmes County so we can spend more time with our family."

Mark's mouth dropped open. "Really, Grandpa? That would be great!"

"Well, don't get too excited, because it hasn't happened yet. We're only in the thinking stages, and if we do make the decision to move, it may not happen until later this year."

"I'm gonna pray that you make that decision," Mark said. "It would be good to have all our grandparents living close by." He picked up his bucket and scurried into the house.

That evening, as everyone sat around the dining room table, Grandma Miller commented on the pretty tulips Mattie had picked and put in a vase.

Mattie smiled. "They came from my own little garden, and I think they're even prettier and more colorful than the ones in Mom's garden."

"Now Mattie," Grandma Troyer spoke up, "it's not good to become prideful and brag about things."

"That's right," Grandma Miller agreed. "Bragging puts the center of attention on you, and being full of pride is hochmut."

Mattie's face heated. She should have known better than to boast about her flowers, but they were so pretty, it was hard not to brag about them. After all, she was the one who had planted the tulips bulbs in the fall. She'd also kept the ground watered and pulled all the weeds in her garden so the flowers would have a better chance to bloom. *Of course,* she reminded herself, *God created the flowers and everything else in the world.*

"It's all right to feel good about what you've accomplished," Grandpa Miller spoke up, "but you should let others compliment you, rather than feeling prideful and boasting about things yourself."

Mattie nodded. "I'll try harder to remember that."

"I would like to look at your garden later on," Grandma Troyer spoke up. "Perhaps tomorrow morning, if not before."

Mattie smiled. "That'll be fine, Grandma. I'm anxious to show you."

"Maybe my frog will show up in the garden while you're there," Mark commented. "I've seen him a few times already this spring, and he likes the little dish I put there, filled with water. Think he enjoys having a place to cool off when it's warm."

"We might see some bunnies, or even their mother, 'cause there's a nest near my garden, too," Mattie said. "I've only seen the one baby bunny, but maybe the others are still hiding."

Grandma Troyer smiled. "Baby rabbits are always so cute."

"This fish we're having is sure good," Grandma Miller said, smiling in Mark's direction.

“Danki,” said Mark.

“We almost didn’t have one of these fish to eat,” Grandpa Troyer said with a wink at Mark. “Why don’t you tell everyone what happened?”

Mark quickly related the story about how Twinkles had stolen the fish from his bucket, but he’d managed to get it back.

Everyone laughed, hearing that.

“Where did you catch the fish?” Grandpa Miller asked. “Was it the same place we went fishing last, or did you go to a different spot?”

Mark grinned widely. “It was at the same pond, and the fish I caught were all fatter and longer than any of John’s.” Mark puffed out his chest.

“Do I detect a bit of hochmut in you also, Mark?” Grandma Miller asked.

Mark hung his head.

“You know,” Grandpa Miller put in, “someday you and Mattie might have to eat humble pie, and it might not go down easy.”

Mattie looked at Mark, and Mark looked at Mattie. “Do you know what that means?” Mattie asked. “Have you ever heard of humble pie?”

Mark shook his head.

“You see,” said Grandpa Miller, “many years ago there was a pie made of less-expensive pieces of meat, and it was called ‘humble pie.’ When a person was forced to eat humble pie, they were humbled and thereby agreed that they were wrong. So eating humble pie means you realize you were wrong in bragging or being prideful, and the consequences caught up with you."

"Your grandpa's right," Dad agreed. "To be humble means not being proud or haughty. Have you ever noticed that the middle letter in pride is *i*? And that, of course, is what pride's all about."

"Pride makes a person think everything is about them and not others," Mom put in.

"In Philippians 2:3 it says: 'Do nothing out of selfish ambition or vain conceit. Rather, in humility value others above yourselves,'" Grandma Miller said. "And in Mark 10:43, when Jesus' disciples argued about who would get the places of honor in heaven, He told them, 'Whoever wants to become great among you must be your servant.'"

"Those are good verses of scripture," Grandpa Miller commented. "It should be our goal to please the Lord and serve others, not gain applause for what we do or what we have."

"I'll try to remember that," the twins said at the same time.

Throughout the rest of their meal, Mattie kept quiet. She was afraid if she said something, she might end up bragging. Mattie was excited, though, when Grandma and Grandpa Troyer announced that they might be moving to Holmes County. From the look on Mom's face, Mattie guessed that she was hoping for that, too. It would be wonderful to have all the grandparents living close by. Maybe their new home would be near enough for Mattie to ride her bike over to visit. She'd have to be patient, though, and see what happened. But she could pray that their move here came true.

After their meal was over and everything had been cleaned up, Mom suggested they take their dessert and go outside. "While we eat it, we can talk more about my mamm and daed's possible move," she said cheerfully.

Mattie was more than willing to go outdoors. Even with the air blowing softly through the open windows, the house was warm inside, and it would be cooler in the yard. The humidity had been low all day, and this was the kind of weather that made Mattie want to be outside every chance she got. She remembered seeing some early fireflies the other night, so maybe she and her siblings could have fun catching some while the grown-ups talked.

While everyone moved outside, Mattie got her cake and took it out to the picnic table.

"This looks appenditlich," Grandma Troyer said when Mattie gave her a piece. "Did you make it yourself?"

Mattie nodded. "It's a German raw apple cake, and I made it for our picnic on the last day of school, but I tripped, and it fell on the floor, so nobody got to eat any."

"I'm glad you made it again," Grandpa Miller said. "Now we'll all have a chance to taste it."

Mattie handed out the rest of the pieces. Then she returned to her seat and waited to eat hers until everyone else had taken a bite. She held her breath in anticipation.

"Mmm. . . This is one fine-tasting cake," Grandpa Troyer said, grinning at Mattie.

Grandma Troyer nodded. "I'll have to get the recipe from you."

Mattie snickered. "But, Grandma, I made the cake from the recipe you gave us some time ago."

Grandma's cheeks turned pink, and she blinked her eyes rapidly. "Ach, I remember that now. But you know what, Mattie? I believe this cake of yours tastes even better than mine."

Mattie smiled. She felt good knowing her cake was being enjoyed by all, but she didn't brag about it. Instead, she merely smiled and said, "I'm glad you like it. Maybe next time I'll make a chocolate cake."

Perry looked over at her and grinned. "*Schocklaad*—that's my favorist kind."

Mom tousled Perry's thick hair. "I think you meant to say that chocolate is your *favorite*, not *favorist*."

Perry bobbed his head eagerly, and everyone laughed. Mattie was glad the evening had gone so well. She looked forward to spending more times like this with her family over the summer months.

Mark finished up his piece of cake, enjoying every last crumb and complimenting Mattie for a job well done. He was glad he'd caught some fish today and had hoped to show his grandparents the nice shiny rocks he'd seen on the way home from school a few weeks ago. Much to his dismay, when he'd finally had the opportunity to go back to collect them, they were gone. He'd seen little indentations in the dirt where the stones had once been, so he figured someone must have taken them. But who?

Guess that's what I get for waiting too long, Mark thought with regret. *Then I went and got sick, which delayed me going after the rocks even longer.* It sure wasn't good to procrastinate. That was another new word Mark had recently learned, but he'd decided to keep that word to himself—at least for now.

Later on, Mark enjoyed watching the sun go down in the west, and as soon as it disappeared over the horizon, the first fireflies made their appearance. Mark helped his younger brother and sister catch them. They all laughed as they cupped the bugs in their hands, and Ada squealed, watching them light up. After holding the fireflies for a spell, Mattie showed Ada and Perry how to hold their palms up and watch the bugs fly off. Mark, along with Calvin, put some of the fireflies in a jar with a lid they'd poked holes in, and they would keep them there for a little while to watch them blink and glow.

Mattie and Russell were coming from opposite directions, both looking up at the same firefly. All of a sudden, they reached for the bug but ended up plowing into each other and landing on the ground.

"Are you okay?" Mom hollered.

"We're fine," Russell said, helping Mattie stand. "But that old firefly sure got away."

Everyone laughed.

Sitting in the lawn chair again, Mark leaned back and sighed deeply. *If only every day could end as good as this one,* he thought.

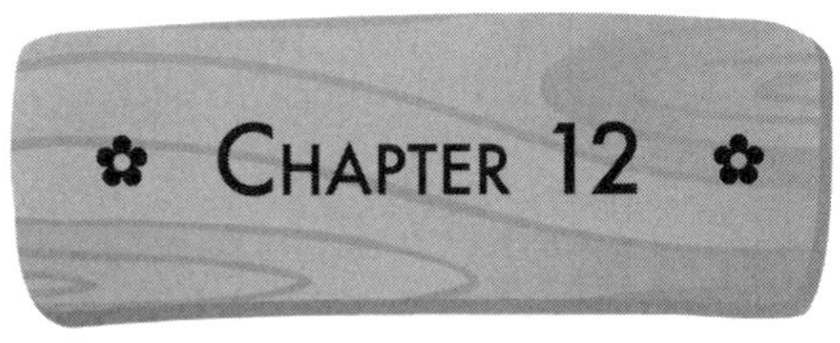

Stella's Visit

By the middle of June, the weather had turned quite warm, but the humidity was still low, so it was easy to be outside.

"Want to shoot some hoops with me?" Mark asked Calvin one morning after they'd eaten breakfast and Mark had finished washing the dishes.

"Can't do it today," Calvin said. "Russell and I are goin' to Millersburg."

"How come?" Mark wanted to know.

"We want to spend the money we've earned helping in Dad's shop, and we enjoy shopping in the big Wal-Mart. Want to go with us, Mark?"

He shook his head. "I don't have any money to spend, and it wouldn't be fun to go along if I couldn't buy anything. Besides, the weather's nice today, and I want to play some basketball."

Calvin gave Mark's shoulder a light thump. "Guess you'd better figure out a way to make some money then, because I'm sure there are some things you'll want to buy this summer."

"That's true." Mark nodded. "Mattie and I will be earning money as soon as we have some things from the garden we can sell at our roadside stand. But that won't be for several more weeks, and I can't think of any other way to make money right now."

"Maybe you can help Dad or Grandpa Miller with yard work," Calvin suggested.

"Jah, maybe so."

"But if I were you, for today anyway, I would just enjoy your time off from school and have fun shooting baskets." Calvin grabbed his straw hat from the wall peg in the utility room and opened the back door. "See you later, Mark."

Mark turned to Mattie, who was still drying the dishes he'd washed. "Do you want to try shooting some hoops?" he asked.

She wrinkled her nose. "I don't think so, Mark. That doesn't sound like fun to me. Besides, I'm planning to teach Twinkles how to ride in the basket of my bike."

"That could be dangerous," Mark cautioned. "If your hund doesn't like it there, she might try to jump out. Or what if you lose your balance on the bike, and it topples over? Poor Twinkles could fall right out."

Mattie sucked in her bottom lip. "Hmm. . . I hadn't thought of that. Maybe teaching Twinkles to ride in the basket isn't such a good idea after all."

Mark moved closer to Mattie. "If you've given up on that idea, then would you at least try shooting some hoops with me? You're good at baseball, so maybe you'll be good at basketball, too."

Mattie picked up a clean bowl and dried it with the dish towel before answering. "Okay, I'll give it a try."

Mattie and Mark had been playing basketball for a while when Stella rode in on her bike. Mattie was glad for the interruption, because she hadn't made any baskets at all. Mark, on the other hand, had made several, and kept bragging about it. Mattie had even reminded him about the verses of scripture Grandma Miller had shared with them, but he kept boasting about how good he was at getting the ball through the hoop. He even said he was better at playing basketball than she was at baseball. Mattie didn't think that was true at all, but she decided not to argue about it. If it made Mark feel better, then let him think whatever he wanted.

"Stella's here now, and I'm sure she came over so we could do something fun together," Mattie said, handing Mark the basketball.

"Does that mean you're quitting?" he asked with a frown.

"Of course that's what it means. I may be good at baseball, but playing basketball isn't for me." Mattie hurried away.

"Wie geht's?" Mattie asked as she approached Stella. "I haven't seen you in a while."

Stella smiled. "I'm fine, and the reason you

haven't seen me is because I went with my family to Pennsylvania for a few weeks."

"Why'd you go there?" Mattie questioned.

"We went to visit my grandparents who live in Bird-in-Hand. We just got back a few days ago, and I've been anxious to see you." Stella motioned to the basket on her bike. "I wanted to show you the pretty rocks I found a few days after school let out."

Mattie moved to the front of Stella's bike and peered into the basket. Inside was a cardboard box filled with several sparkly rocks. "Wow, those are sure pretty felse."

"Take one out. You can have it if you like," Stella said.

Mattie wasn't that interested in rocks, but these were different than most she'd seen, and she thought it might be nice to have one she could set on the dresser in her room. "Danki, Stella," she said, reaching inside and taking one of the sparkling rocks.

"Say, where'd you get those?" Mark asked, joining the girls by Stella's bike. Mattie was surprised that he wasn't still practicing his basketball skills.

"Found a bunch of pretty rocks on the path near our school," Stella replied. "Aren't they nice?"

Mark held his lips tightly together as he slowly shook his head.

"What's wrong?" Stella questioned. "Don't you like my rocks?"

"I like 'em just fine," Mark said, "but they were supposed to be mine."

Stella tipped her head. “What do you mean?”

“I spotted a bunch of sparkly rocks on the way to school one day, but due to the rainy weather and then me getting sick with the flu, I never got the chance to go back and get them. Then after I got better, I kept procrastinating.”

“Procrasti—what?” Stella asked with a curious expression.

“Procrastinating. It means to put off doing something,” Mark explained.

“Oh, I see. That’s a pretty big word, if you ask me.”

“Jah, it is, but it’s okay, ’cause I like saying big words.”

Mattie rolled her eyes. She figured Mark was just showing off.

“Then when I did finally go back to get the rocks, they were gone,” Mark continued. His forehead wrinkled. “Now I know why. It’s ’cause you got ’em all.”

“I can see that you’re disappointed,” Stella said, “but I had no way of knowing you’d seen the rocks first.” She reached into her basket and took out two of the rocks. “Here, why don’t you add these to your collection?”

Mark hesitated, but then he smiled and said, “Danki, Stella. It’s not the same as gettin’ all the pretty felse, but I appreciate the two you gave me.”

“You didn’t need all the rocks anyway,” Mattie said. “You already have a lot of rocks.”

“That’s true, but since Dad helped me make a big wooden box to store them all in, I have room for plenty more," Mark replied, smiling widely.

"You must have a lot of rocks if you need a big wooden box." Stella's eyebrows rose.

He grinned. "I sure do, and I hope to find even more."

Mattie rolled her eyes once more. Some of her brother's rocks were pretty, but she didn't understand why he needed so many.

"Hey, look at that. I just saw a little chickadee go into your birdhouse over there," Stella said excitedly.

Mattie and Mark looked in the direction Stella was pointing.

"Maybe it's gonna build a nest in there," Mattie said. "We had bluebird babies in the birdhouse earlier this spring."

"Jah," Mark piped up. "They fledged about three weeks ago."

"Fledged?" Stella looked at Mark strangely. "What does that mean?"

"Here we go again," Mattie mumbled under her breath.

"It means that a young bird has fully developed feathers and wing muscles, making it able to fly," Mark explained.

"Once all the baby birds left the nest, we cleaned out the birdhouse right away, hoping another bird might build a nest inside," Mattie added.

"Well, it looks like you might get your wish." Stella pointed again. "See there? A second bird just joined the first chickadee."

The three of them watched for a while as the birds scouted for material, taking turns going in and out of the birdhouse to prepare a new nest inside.

"Stella, why don't we sit on the porch swing awhile?" Mattie suggested. "I'm tired of watching the birds. We can visit now, and you can tell me all about your trip to Pennsylvania."

"Sure, I'd be happy to tell you about it." Stella nodded.

"Mind if I join you?" Mark asked. "I'd like to hear about Pennsylvania, too."

Mattie wished Mark would find something else to do. After all, Stella was her best friend, not his. But she didn't want to hurt her brother's feelings, so she smiled and said, "If Stella's okay with it, then I am, too."

Mark looked at Stella, and she smiled at him. "It's fine with me if you want to sit with us and hear about my trip."

Mark had just taken a seat on the wicker chair near the swing, to listen to Stella talk about the faceless doll she'd bought when they were in Pennsylvania, when he felt something tug on his shoe. He looked down and saw Twinkles with his shoelace in her mouth.

"Hey!" Mark shouted. "Let go of my *schuhbendel*!"

Twinkles didn't let go. Instead, she started shaking her head back and forth, while tugging on Mark's shoelace all the more.

"Make her stop, Mattie," Mark shouted. "Make her stop right now!"

Mattie clapped her hands loudly. "Twinkles, let go of Mark's shoelace!"

The naughty little dog kept pulling and shaking her head, and now she was growling. It seemed like Twinkles was having a contest with Mark's shoe.

Stella started to giggle, which made things even worse, because Mark didn't think it was one bit funny. He didn't think Mattie's friend would laugh if Twinkles were trying to eat her shoelace.

"Sorry," Stella said, covering her mouth with her hand. "Mattie's silly hund looks so funny trying to eat your shoelace, I couldn't help but laugh."

The wind whipped up just then and whistled under the roof of the porch. Suddenly, Twinkles let go of Mark's shoelace and darted into the yard. *Gr-r-r-r! Gr-r-r-r!* The hair on her back stood straight up as she growled and barked.

"What's wrong with Twinkles?" Stella asked. "Is she afraid because it's *wendich*?"

"I don't think she's growling because it's windy." Mattie pointed across the yard. "I think she's afraid of that plastic bag blowing down the driveway."

Mark reached down and retied his shoe. "Well, at least she let go of my schuhbendel and found something else to do."

"Look over there!" Stella laughed and pointed to one

of the bird feeders in their yard. "See that silly squirrel trying to eat the food that's meant for the birds?"

Mark and Mattie looked, and they began to laugh, too. The feeder was one that Grandpa Miller had made, and he called it "the whirlwind." Birds could perch on it and eat with no problem because they didn't weigh much, but it wasn't made for a squirrel. If a larger animal got on the feeder, it would spin and eventually send the critter flying off, which was exactly what happened to this poor little squirrel. Round and round it went, spinning full circle, like a merry-go-round. After several more spins, and hanging on for dear life, it couldn't hold on any longer and went sailing through the air. The critter landed in some tall grass. A few seconds later, it got up and zipped right over the fence.

Mark sighed with relief. He was glad the little fellow wasn't hurt. Hopefully, it had learned a lesson and wouldn't try to eat the birds' food again.

Mark looked at Mattie, and she looked at Stella, and they started to giggle again. They laughed so hard, they had to bend over and hold their sides. Mark thought it was nice to have a little fun with his twin sister and her best friend. He hoped they'd have lots more things to laugh about throughout the summer.

"Say," Mattie spoke up when they'd finally quit laughing, "I made some *kichlin* last night, and they're really good. Should I bring some out so we can have a snack while you tell us about your trip to Pennsylvania?"

"That's sounds nice," Stella said. "I'd like to try a few of your cookies."

"You're in for a treat." Mattie smiled. "They're chocolate chip, and I think they are better than any kichlin I've ever tasted before."

Mark bumped his sister's arm. "That's sounds like bragging, Mattie. Remember, it's not good to be prideful."

"Jah, I know. Danki for the reminder, Mark."

"Why don't I go in the house and get the cookies for us to eat?" Mark asked, rising to his feet. "That way, you can sit here and visit with Stella some more."

"That's nice of you," Mattie replied, "but don't you want to hear about Stella's trip?"

"She can tell me about it when I come back outside." Mark hurried into the house, feeling good that he'd done something nice and hadn't boasted about it.

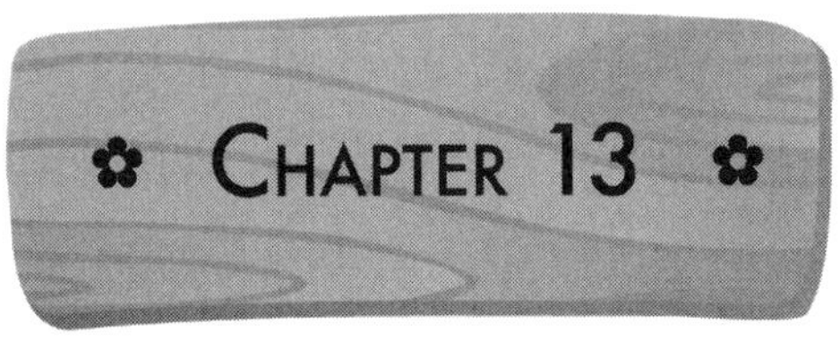

A Bat to Catch

"Sure is a warm day," Mattie complained as she and Mark sat behind their parents' produce stand near the end of their driveway one morning in early July. In a matter of a few weeks, it had really warmed up, and like most days in July, the humidity had set in.

Looking across the road, and even back to their house, it appeared as if fog had settled across the land. Even the sun looked milky in the hazy sky. They'd been here for almost an hour and had only sold a few things from Mom's vegetable garden. The air was so uncomfortable that just sitting there made Mark and Mattie sweat.

"I know it's hot, but if we make enough money, we'll be able to buy some things we want," Mark said, looking at her with an encouraging expression.

"That's what I'm hoping for, but we need more customers if we're gonna make enough money." Mattie leaned back in her chair, staring at the road, wishing and praying for more customers to stop by. "I'd like to buy some colored pencils and a new drawing tablet," she said.

"I'm hoping to get a new light and also a basket for my bike," Mark said.

"But you already have a basket," Mattie reminded him, waving her hand to stir up some air.

"It's not big enough. I need more room for the felse I find when I go rock hunting."

Mattie shrugged her shoulders. "That's up to you, but I think the basket you have on your bike is big enough."

"You can think whatever you like," Mark said, "but if I earn enough money I'm gonna buy whatever I want."

"Maybe I should have picked some blumme from my garden to sell," Mattie commented. "Wouldn't that be great if the flowers made us more money?"

"Jah, but you didn't pick any, and I don't want to sit here in the hot sun by myself while you run back to the yard to pick blumme."

"If we come back here tomorrow, I'll bring some," Mattie said. "Know what I wish we could do today?"

"What?"

"I'd like to have a water balloon fight. Since it's so hot, the *wasser* would help to cool us down."

"The little bit of water inside the balloons wouldn't cool us nearly as well as if we went swimming in the pond." Mark removed his straw hat and fanned his face with the brim. "Maybe one of us should go up to the house and ask Mom if we can go swimming."

"I don't think she'd let us," Mattie said. "We're supposed to try and sell all this produce, and if we went swimming today, nothing would get sold."

"Well, we need to have more customers in order for anything to sell." Mark groaned, leaning his elbows on the wooden counter. "This is so monotonous, and I'm getting tired of just sitting here, waiting." He reached up and touched the back of his neck. "I can feel the sweat running from my neck all the way down my back."

"I know, 'cause I'm all sweaty, too. And by the way. . . What's the word *monotonous* mean?" Mattie questioned. "Don't think I've ever heard it before."

"It means boring," Mark explained. "And I'm plenty bored right now, aren't you?"

"Jah, but there's not much for us to do except sit here and wait for someone to show up."

"We could play a word game," Mark suggested.

Mattie sighed. "I don't like your word games. They're always hard."

"Not for me," he said with a shake of his head. "I'm really good with words, and I'll bet I know more big words than any of our older brieder. Maybe more than Mom or Dad, too." Mark puffed out his chest and lifted his chin. "Grandpa Miller knows a lot of big words, and I'm happy to say that I take after him."

Mattie nudged her brother's arm. "Are you bragging again, Mark?"

"I'm not braggin'; just stating facts."

"Humph! Sounded to me like you were bragging. Don't you remember what we've learned about that? I don't think boasting about ourselves is pleasing to God, and I'm trying to do better about that."

Mark frowned. "I don't think you ought to be givin' me a lecture. You're not my mamm or one of the ministers in our church, you know."

"No, I'm your twin sister, and I just think—"

A horse and buggy pulled in, and a middle-aged Amish woman got out. Mattie didn't recognize her and figured she must be from another church district.

The woman tied her horse to the fence post and walked over to their produce stand. "Do you have any dill weed for sale?" she asked.

Mattie shook her head. "Sorry, but our mamm didn't grow any dill weed in her garden this year."

"That's too bad," the woman said. "I need some for the dilled green beans I am going to can. Guess I'll look at another produce stand on down the road." As she turned to go, Mattie caught sight of a garter snake slithering through the grass. Closer and closer it came to the woman's shoe, until it was just a few inches away. Mattie was afraid if the woman took one more step, she would hurt the little snake, so she knew she had to do something real quick.

"Please, don't move," Mattie said calmly, so as not to frighten the woman. "There's a *schlang* by your foot."

"A snake? I—I don't like snakes!" The woman's eyes widened, and she jumped back, just missing the reptile. Without another word, she turned and ran back to her buggy.

"It's okay. It's only a garter snake," Mattie called, but it was too late. The woman had already untied the horse and climbed into her buggy.

Mattie stepped out from behind the stand and picked up the snake.

"Yikes! Don't bring that schlang anywhere near me!" Mark shouted, standing up on his stool.

Mattie knew her twin brother was afraid of snakes, but she didn't think he would freak out like that.

"Don't worry. The snake won't hurt you," Mattie said, stroking the top of the creature's head. "Garter snakes are harmless to humans. They're good for getting bugs, though, so I think I'll put him in Mom's garden where he can do what he does best."

"Oh, great," Mark said. "Now Mom will probably see the schlang when she's out there weeding. I bet she won't like that at all. And you know what else?" Mark asked with his hands on his hips. "That snake might eat my frog, or any other frog that shows up to sit in the pool inside your garden."

"Have you seen any more frogs this summer yet, swimming around in that little dish pond of yours?" Mattie questioned.

"I did earlier this spring, but I haven't seen any since then." Mark frowned. "But if any frogs are nearby, I don't want some old snake to scare them off—or worse yet, try to eat 'em."

Mattie remembered back to the time she'd put a fake snake in Mark's bed. When Mom found it in the laundry basket, she'd gotten real upset. A snake could scare the rabbit family, and if a snake ate one of Mark's frogs, that would bad, too. "Well, maybe I'll just put it over there in the weeds," Mattie said.

After Mattie placed the snake in the weeds near the fence, she returned to the produce stand. Mark had climbed down off the stool and was sitting on it again.

"Don't know why you're so afraid of a schlang," Mattie said, seating herself beside him. "I think they're quite interesting."

"Don't see what's so interesting about snakes," he said, folding his arms.

Mattie held up her index finger. "One interesting fact is that they have no limbs."

Mark merely shrugged in response.

Mattie held up a second finger. "Another curious thing is that snakes are cold-blooded, so they regulate their body temperature by basking in the sunlight for a while to warm up and then moving on to a shady spot to cool down. They also shed their skin and hibernate."

Mark tipped his head and looked at Mattie strangely. "Have you been looking in my encyclopedia? Is that how you know so much about snakes?"

She shook her head. "I read it in a magazine at the dentist's office the last time I was there. Don't you think what I told you about snakes is interesting?"

He shook his head. "What I think is that you're just trying to prove how schmaert you are. Maybe you even think you're smarter than me."

"I do not," Mattie defended. "I just know some stuff you don't know, and you know things I don't. Besides, our differences are what make us unique. We could actually teach each other some interesting facts about different things. Is there anything wrong with that?"

"No, I guess not. Sorry, Mattie. I'm just feelin' kind of crabby right now 'cause it's hot out here and we're not making much money."

Mattie wiped a trickle of sweat from her forehead and sighed. "Maybe things will go better after lunch."

"I sure hope so." Mark reached under the stand where they'd put their lunch pails and pulled his out. "Think I'm gonna eat mine right now."

"Me too," Mattie said, removing her lunch pail as well.

The twins had just started eating, when Calvin came out of the barn, pulling their little red wagon. Perry was with him. "Mom says it's too hot out here right now and that you should put the vegetables in the wagon and come inside for a glass of cold lemonade." Calvin positioned the wagon in front of the stand. "I'll help you with it."

"You just missed seeing a garter snake," Mattie said. "Bet you would have liked it, Perry."

Perry's eyes widened. "A schlang? Where did it go, Mattie?"

"Slithered off into the tall grass," Mattie replied.

"I'm sure it's long gone by now."

Perry frowned. "I always miss all the fun."

"There's nothing fun about a snake," Mark said, closing his lunch pail and going around to help Calvin load the wagon. "It's sure a disappointment that we didn't sell much today," he muttered. "I wish the weather wasn't so hot. I'm sure it's keeping customers away."

"We'll try again tomorrow, or some other day," Mattie said. "Just think of it this way: we don't have to sit out here all day and sweat. We can go inside and drink some of Mom's sweet lemonade."

"That's true," Mark agreed. "So let's get all these vegetables loaded in the wagon and take them up to the house."

That evening, as Mark was getting ready for bed, he heard a strange noise outside his bedroom door. At the same time, he thought he heard a frog croaking outside, close to the house.

He moved across the room and stood by the open window. Sure enough, over toward Mattie's flower bed, where he'd placed the ceramic pool, he heard a *ribbet-ribbet.*

"Oh, good," Mark said aloud. "Looks like Hoppy the Frog is back in Mattie's garden." If it wasn't so dark, he would tiptoe downstairs and go outside to get a look at the frog.

Maybe I'll get my flashlight and go anyway, he thought.

Just as Mark was about to open his dresser drawer, he heard that strange noise in the hallway again.

Holding very still, he tipped his head and listened intently. Then he put his ear up against the door. It was a swooshing sound, and he just had to find out what it was.

Cautiously, Mark opened the door and peered out. It was dark, and he couldn't see much of anything. Then he felt something brush the top of his head. He gulped and ducked. *What was that?* he wondered. *Could someone have left a window or door open and a bird got into our house?*

Mark went back to his room and grabbed a flashlight. When he stepped into the hall again and turned on his light, he was surprised to see a furry little bat swooping from one end of the hallway to the other.

The door to Mattie's room opened just then. "What's going on out here?" she questioned. "I heard a weird kind of noise."

"I heard it, too, and it's a bat." Mark shined the light upward again. "See there."

Mattie gasped and crouched low to the floor. "Ach, Mark, how are we gonna get the bat out of the house?"

"You're not scared of it, are you, Mattie?" Mark asked, already knowing the answer. His twin sister was not only down on the floor, but she'd begun to cry. "Come on, Mattie, don't be afraid. It's not the first time we've had a bat in the house."

"I don't care. One time was enough. Call Dad, Mark," Mattie whimpered. "Call Dad to come upstairs and get the bat out."

Whoosh! With flapping wings, the bat made another pass over Mark's head. He didn't want to hurt the bat but needed to get it out of the house. He could either call Dad, like Mattie said, or try to capture the bat himself.

"I'll be right back," Mark said.

"Where are you going?" Mattie asked, looking up at the bat, now clinging to the ceiling.

"To my room," he answered. "I'm gonna look for something to help me capture the bat."

"Don't leave me out here with that creature," Mattie said. "I'm scared."

"Go back to your room then and shut the door," Mark told her. "I'll let you know when the bat is gone."

"No problem. That critter is creepy."

As Mattie crept back to her room, Mark stepped into his room and grabbed a blanket.

He was surprised that Mattie was afraid of the bat, especially because last year they'd had an incident with a bat, only that one had been caught in the living-room curtain. Mattie's reaction to the bat made Mark feel a little better about his fear of snakes. He guessed everyone had something they were afraid of. Mark remembered Dad saying once that it was important not to let fear take over your thoughts. From now on, whenever Mark saw a snake, he would try to be a little braver about it. Right now, though, he had a bat to catch.

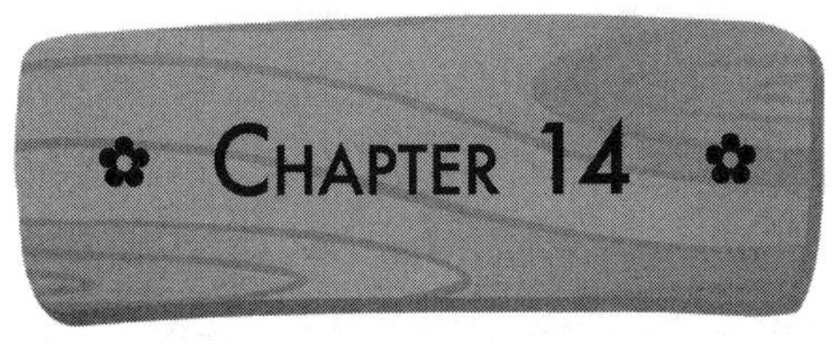

Broken Latch

Mattie sat on the edge of her bed and shivered. She couldn't believe Mark was out there alone with that bat. Wasn't he afraid it might bite him? What if it had rabies? He really ought to call on Dad or one of the brothers to help. Is he really that brave or just showing off?

Mattie was tempted to peek out her door and see how things were going, but she was too scared. What if the bat flew into her room when she opened the bedroom door? She didn't know what she would do then.

How are these bats getting into our house? Mattie wondered. *Maybe Dad can figure it out so it won't happen again.*

Mattie didn't want to take any chances. What if, somehow, that bat had gotten in through one of their windows? From now on, she'd make sure to keep hers closed until Dad had a chance to make sure all the screens were secure. Even though it was a warm night,

Mattie hurried to her window and shut it tight. Then she went back and sat on the edge of her bed, listening and waiting to find out what would happen out in the hall. She was ever so thankful that the bat wasn't in her room. If it had been, she would have panicked.

Mattie rubbed her goose-bumped arms. If that varmint had gotten into her room, it could have crawled on her while she was sleeping. *Eww*. . . She couldn't help squirming just thinking about it. For now, though, she would sit here and pray for Mark.

Mark couldn't believe how quickly that little bat flew back and forth. *If I only had a net,* he thought. *I'd have no trouble getting the bat. Guess this blanket will have to do.* Mark thought if he could catch the critter all by himself, it would be something exciting to tell his family and friends about.

The bat made another pass over Mark's head, and he leaped into the air with the blanket. But instead of trapping the bat as he'd hoped, Mark tripped on the edge of the blanket and fell with a *thunk*!

A few seconds later, Russell, Calvin, and Ike came out of their rooms. "What's going on out here?" Russell asked, yawning and rubbing his eyes. "I'd just gotten to sleep when I heard a *thunk* and woke up."

"There's a bat in the house, and I'm tryin' to catch it." Mark untangled his feet and pointed to where he'd last seen the critter. "It was right up in that area. Can't believe another bat has gotten into our house."

"We need more light so we can see him better," Ike said. "I'll get my flashlight and the gas lamp from the bathroom."

"Russell and I have flashlights we can use, too," Calvin said. "We'll get them right now."

While Mark waited for his brothers to return, he continued to chase the bat. It was as though the winged creature was playing a game, letting Mark get close and then at the last minute, escaping the blanket's capture.

Calvin, Russell, and Ike returned with their lights and joined the chase, but the tricky little critter kept out of their reach.

A few minutes later, Dad came up the stairs. "What are you boys doing out of bed? With all that racket you made, you woke your mamm and me." He frowned. "The next thing you know, Perry and Ada will be up, too," he said in a low, but stern voice. "Now what's going on?"

"Another bat has gotten into the house, and it's been flying back and forth in the hallway up here," Mark explained. "I've been trying to capture him in a blanket, but he's too schmaert for me."

"Hang on. I'll be right back," Dad said before tiptoeing back down the stairs. When he returned, he had a broom.

"What are you going to do with that?" Mark

questioned, feeling concern. "You're not gonna kill the bat, I hope."

Dad shook his head. "I'll just hit it gently and knock it to the ground. Then we'll capture the bat in the blanket and take it outside."

"Oh, okay." Mark watched as the bat made another pass, and he held his breath when Dad swatted the bat with the broom. One gentle swing was all it took, and the bat dropped to the floor.

"Is it dead?" Calvin wanted to know.

"I don't think so. Just a little stunned," Dad said. "Let's get the bat in the blanket and take it outside. In the morning, I'll check the screens in all our windows to make sure they're secure. If I find any loose screens, I'll fix them, and that should keep more bats from getting in."

Dad scooped up the bat, using the broom, and placed it on the blanket, which Mark had laid on the floor. Then Mark quickly folded the edges of the blanket over the bat. When that was done, Dad picked it up and started downstairs. "You can all go back to bed now," he called over his shoulder. "Morning comes early, you know."

"Can I come with you, Dad?" Mark asked as his brothers returned to their rooms. "I'd like to see if the bat's okay."

"Jah, sure," Dad said.

Once they were outside, Dad opened the blanket and shook the bat out. It lay on the ground unmoving, and Mark was almost certain it was dead. A few minutes went by, and the bat moved its small wings. Then, with a flutter, it flew off into the night sky.

"Whew!" Mark exclaimed. "That's a relief."

Dad smiled and gave Mark's shoulder a squeeze. "Now take this blanket and put it in the laundry room. Your mamm will want to wash it in the morning."

Mark did as Dad asked, and after he'd headed upstairs to his room, he decided to stop and talk to Mattie. He figured with all the commotion going on, she was probably still awake and wondering about the bat.

Tap! Tap! Mark rapped softly on Mattie's door. "Mattie, it's me. Is it okay if I come in?"

"Sure," she responded.

When Mark entered Mattie's room, he shined his flashlight and saw that she was sitting on the edge of her bed, wide-eyed and trembling.

"The bat's gone now, so you can relax." Mark took a seat beside his sister and patted her hand. "It was a little brown bat like the one that got in our house before."

"Is. . .is it dead?"

"Nope. Dad took it outside, and it flew off into the night."

"I'm glad the bat is okay," Mattie said, "even though it was creepy."

Mark looked at Mattie's window. "It's sure stuffy in here. How come your window is shut?"

"I know it may seem silly to you," Mattie said, "but those things creep me out. I was worried that the bat may have come through my window somehow."

Mark walked over and opened Mattie's window. "I don't think you have to worry about that. The screen is in good condition and would keep a bat out. Dad's gonna check all the window screens tomorrow, but I've been thinkin' that the bat may have flown into the house when one of us opened the door to come in from outside."

"Guess that could have happened, all right. We'll have to be more careful," Mattie said. "I couldn't stand it if another bat got in."

"I understand," he said. "You don't like bats, and I don't like snakes."

"That's true," she agreed. "Just like everyone has certain things they enjoy, we each have things we don't care for, either."

Mark nodded. "Guess I'd better get to bed." He yawned. "I feel some cool air coming into your room now. Sleep well, Mattie."

"I'll try, and I hope I don't have a bad dream about that crazy bat. You sleep well, too, Mark. See you in the morning."

As Mark slipped out of Mattie's room and across the hall to his own, he smiled. Tomorrow was bound to be a better day, because it was Saturday, and Dad said he would take the whole family to the fund-raising auction in Mt. Hope. The money that came in for the things that would be auctioned off would go to help some Amish families with their medical bills. Mark looked forward to going.

The next morning after breakfast, Mark went to the barn to feed his cats. Lucky and Boots greeted him with loud *meows* and rubbed against his legs. Mark bent down to pet the cats, and they both began to purr.

He smiled. "I'll bet you two are hungerich and just waiting to be fed, aren't ya?"

The cats responded with more purring, and then they both took off. When they came to their empty dishes, they meowed even louder.

"Okay, okay," Mark said as he took down their food. "You two are so impatient."

After Mark poured food into the cats' dishes, he put the bag away and walked over to the horses' stalls to say good morning and see how they were doing. Dad's buggy horse was not in his stall, since Ike had come out earlier and gotten the horse so he could hitch him to Dad's market buggy. Ike's and Mom's horses were still in their stalls, so Mark took a few minutes to stroke their noses and give them both a few lumps of sugar.

Mom's horse nuzzled Mark's hand and let out a loud *Neigh! Neigh!* Ike's horse swished his tail and slobbered on Mark's hand.

"Yuck! I didn't ask for that," Mark muttered, wiping his hand on a rag.

He was about to leave when he noticed that the

latch on Mom's horse's stall was broken and the door wouldn't stay tightly closed.

I'll have to tell Dad about that, Mark told himself. In the meantime, he found a thin piece of rope and tied the gate shut. "That oughta hold till Dad can get the gate fixed properly," Mark said.

Eager to get outside and see if everyone was ready for their trip to Mt. Hope, Mark hurried from the barn. He loved going to the auction. Lots of people would be there, and he always found so much to see. Mattie and Mom would enjoy all the flowers and produce. Livestock, such as draft horses, buggy horses, cattle, pigs, and goats, would be auctioned off. What Mark looked forward to the most, though, was all the good-smelling food, and he couldn't wait to see what all would be there to eat.

Chapter 15

Blueberry Pie

"Are you excited about going to the auction?" Mattie asked Mark as they sat with Perry on the bench in the back of Dad's market buggy.

He bobbed his head with an eager expression. "Sure hope there's lots of good food."

Mattie rolled her eyes. "We just had breakfast not long ago, and you're already thinking about food?"

Mark thumped his stomach. "If I want to keep growing taller, I need lots to eat. And I'm sure the food will be good. Bet I can eat more than you do, Mattie."

She nudged his arm. "You'll get wider, not taller, if you eat too much, and you're being prideful, Brother."

"Besides that, you might get sick to your stomach," Perry chimed in. He sat on the other side of Mark, and Ada was seated up front between Mom and Dad. Since Ike had taken his own horse and buggy, Calvin and Russell rode with him. That left plenty of room in the back of Dad's buggy for Mark, Mattie, and Perry.

"I won't overeat," Mark said, "but I will enjoy a hot

dog with lots of ketchup, and maybe an ice-cream cone."

Perry smacked his lips. "Yum. I want some ice cream, too."

"How about you, Mattie?" Mark asked. "Are you hoping there will be ice cream there to buy?"

"Jah, sure," she replied. "Cold vanilla ice cream's always good on a hot day like this, and it's one of my favorites." Mattie fanned her face with her hand. She loved going on family outings like this but wished the weather was cooler. Here it was only morning, and already it was hotter than yesterday had been. As the sun went higher into the steamy sky, the temperature and humidity rose. They would need to drink lots of water and stay in the shade as much as possible, because they didn't want to get dehydrated. She'd heard that word from Grandpa Miller. *Guess Mark's not the only one who can learn big words,* Mattie thought, smiling to herself.

As they headed down the road, Mattie yawned. Not only did the heat make her tired, but hearing the rhythmic *clip-clop* of the horse's hooves and rocking with the motion of the buggy relaxed her enough that she could fall asleep in minutes. Also, she was extremely tired this morning, because after the bat ordeal last night she hadn't slept well. With all the commotion, it had taken her a long time to fall asleep. When Mark reopened her window, that helped to cool her room a bit, but she'd huddled fearfully under her blankets. It was uncomfortable, and a little too hot, but at least she'd felt protected from unseen things in the night. Once Mattie did fall asleep, a nightmare about a bat woke her up again. Finally, after imagining all sorts of noises, Mattie had drifted into slumber sometime during the wee hours of the morning. Now, with the motion of the buggy, she fought the urge to doze off and tried to concentrate on the scenery as they rode by, so she could stay awake.

When they arrived at the auction and everyone had gotten out of the buggy, Dad parked the rig in the shaded area reserved for buggies, and tied their horse to a hitching rail. Then everyone walked toward the big auction barn. So many people were milling around the place, with lots to see. The English as well as the Amish had come from all over to witness and take part in the events. Mattie hoped Stella and her family would be here, but so far she'd seen no sign of them.

They met up with Ike, Calvin, and Russell for a bit, but then the brothers headed off to take in the sights and visit with some of their friends.

"Your daed and I are going in the barn to see what all is being auctioned off," Mom said, looking at Mattie. "You and Mark can walk around and look at things out here if you like."

"What about Ada and Perry?" Mattie questioned. "Are they going with you and Dad?"

Mom pursed her lips. "Well, I'd hoped you and Mark might take them along with you. They might get bored and restless in the auction barn."

"Jah, okay." Mattie wasn't thrilled about having her little brother and sister tag along, but she needed to do as her mother asked. Since Ike, Calvin, and Russell had already gone their own way, Ada and Perry couldn't go with them.

Mattie took Ada's hand, and Mark took Perry's. They said good-bye to their folks and headed off to look at some baby animals. They'd only gone a short ways when Mattie spotted Grandpa and Grandma Miller walking toward them.

"*Guder mariye,*" Grandma said, smiling.

"Good morning," Mattie and Mark replied at the same time.

"Where's your mamm and daed?" Grandpa asked.

"Our older brieder went to look at the bulls, and Mom and Dad headed to the auction barn," Mark answered, pointing toward it.

"That's where I'm going," Grandpa said.

"What about you, Grandma?" Mattie asked.

Grandma smiled. "I thought I'd walk around for a while. Maybe see who's selling what at some of the booths nearby. I'd like to see what flowers are for sale, too."

"Would you mind if Ada and Perry tag along with you?" Mattie questioned.

"That's a good idea," Mark put in.

Perry frowned. "But I wanna go with you and Mattie."

Ada grabbed hold of Grandma's hand. It was

obvious that she'd rather spend time with her then be with Mark and Mattie.

"I'll tell you what," Grandma said, looking at Perry. "If you come along with me and Ada, I'll buy you both a balloon."

Perry's eyes brightened. "Okay!"

Ada clapped her hands and wiggled around.

Mattie sighed with relief. It would have been hard for her and Mark to see and do much if they had to keep an eye on their little sister and brother. Besides, Ada and Perry would probably have a better time with Grandma—especially since she'd offered to buy them balloons.

With the little ones walking close beside her, Grandma headed one way, and Mark and Mattie went the other.

"Hey, look at that!" Mark pointed to some pamphlets lying on the end of a table.

They both ran over and picked one up. "I don't see anything interesting," Mattie said, looking at her brother, while adjusting her head covering.

"It says that there's gonna be a bird-and-animal sale in September." Mark pointed to a section in the flyer. "I hope we can come to that auction, too."

"They have animal sales here just about every week," Mattie reminded him. "What's so different about the one coming in September?"

"From what I'm reading, it's not for livestock. This one will be for domestic and exotic animals and birds," Mark said.

Mattie read more closely. "You're right. It says here that they'll be auctioning off buffalo, elk, and deer. Even some camels and zebras."

"Read further. There'll be llamas, alpacas, quail, hamsters, guinea pigs, doves, and even some pot-bellied pigs. I wonder if we'd be allowed to have one of those."

"One what?" Mattie asked her brother.

"A hamster or a guinea pig. They even have some flying squirrels listed, too," Mark exclaimed. "Wow, I really hope we get to come to that sale in September. Wouldn't it be great to see all those critters?"

"I guess, but I don't think I'd want to have any of them as pets. I'm satisfied with Twinkles, and you should be content with your katze."

"You're probably right, but it'd still be fun to see all those different animals and birds."

Mattie and Mark continued on. They walked past several booths selling various food items, until they came to a sign that read: PIE-EATING CONTEST.

"Oh, boy, look at that!" Mark exclaimed. "I'm hungerich and know I can eat lots of pie, so maybe I should enter the contest."

"That's not a good idea," Mattie said.

"Why not?"

"If you eat too much pie, you won't have room for lunch." Mattie stared at all the pies sitting on a long table. She wasn't sure what kind they were, but they had lots of whipped cream on top. "Eating those pies will also be messy," she cautioned.

"I'm sure they'll give everyone a bib or some kind of apron to wear." Mark tugged on Mattie's arm. "Come on, Mattie, let's enter the contest together. It'll be more fun that way, and with both of us entering, we'll have two chances to win instead of one."

Mattie rubbed her chin thoughtfully, pondering the situation. "I don't know, Mark. . . ."

He pointed to another sign at the other end of the table. "Look at the prize the one who eats the most will get. Don't you think Mom and Dad would be happy if you or I won that?"

Mattie stared at the sign. It said that whoever ate the most pies in fifteen minutes would win a gift certificate to the Walnut Creek Cheese Store. Mom and Dad shopped there a lot, and Mattie knew they'd be glad to have the gift certificate. Even so, she wasn't sure she wanted to gorge herself on pie, and it would end up being quite messy, even with a bib or apron. She could see doing it if there was a prize she wanted, but not just for a certificate to the cheese store.

"Mattie, come on," Mark insisted, guiding her toward the table. "Looks like they're getting ready to start, and we don't wanna miss out."

These pies do look tasty, Mattie thought, *and it would be nice if one of us could win that prize.*

"Oh, all right," Mattie finally agreed. "After all, how hard can it be?

✿

As Mark and Mattie sat at the table with the other children who were participating in the pie-eating contest, Mattie wondered why she'd agreed to take part in this. There were so many pies. She was sure she could never eat one, let alone eat the most in fifteen minutes.

Each contestant had been given a bib to wear around their neck, and they were told by the judges that they could not use their hands to eat the pies. That meant they had to lean over and eat the pies with only their mouths. One of the judges also said that if they spit any of the pie out, instead of swallowing it, they'd be disqualified.

I should never have let Mark talk me into this, Mattie thought, looking over at him.

Mark looked back at her with a big grin. "I'm gonna win this contest, just wait and see. I'll not only get that prize for Mom and Dad, but winning will prove that I'm the best pie-eater in the whole state of Ohio."

Mattie slowly shook her head. *Here he goes, bragging again. Does it really matter whether he wins or not?*

Someone blew a whistle, letting them know it was time to start. Mattie leaned over and began eating the pie in front of her, and Mark did the same. Mattie liked all kinds of pies, and she was glad this one was blueberry. It was messy, but very good. By the time Mattie finished her first pie, she was full and knew she couldn't eat another bite. She also had whipped cream all over her face.

Mattie stopped eating and turned to watch Mark. He'd finished his first pie and was halfway through a second one. His face was also covered with whipping cream, and purple blueberry juice was all around his mouth. But Mark didn't seem ready to quit. Instead, he wore a determined look. *Chomp! Chomp! Slurp! Slurp!* Mark continued to eat the pie. When the second pie was done, he started the third.

The people standing around began to clap and cheer, which seemed to encourage Mark all the more.

An elderly English man standing nearby laughed so hard tears ran down his cheeks.

"I can do this," Mark said, gasping for breath. "I'm gonna win this contest."

As the crowd urged them on, the English boy next to Mark also started eating a third pie. He chomped and slurped, and every once in a while, he would look at Mark.

Mattie cringed when Mark started on his fourth pie, and by the time he finished that, she was sure he would quit. But her twin brother kept going until the whistle blew. By that time, he was halfway through pie number five. The other boy, who looked a little older than Mark, had eaten a little more pie than Mark, and the judges announced that he was the winner.

"Oh, no," Mark groaned. "I ate all that for nothing, and now I've got a *bauchweh*."

Guess a stomachache is what you get for bragging about how much pie you could eat, Mattie thought. Even so, she felt sorry for Mark. "Come on," she said, leading her brother away from the table. "You need to get cleaned up because your face is a mess."

Mark grimaced and held his stomach. "Don't think I'll ever be able to eat another blueberry pie."

"I think what you ate was some humble pie," Mattie said.

"What do you mean?" he asked.

"Remember when Grandpa Miller said if we kept on bragging we'd someday have to eat humble pie?"

Mark nodded slowly.

"Well, I think that's what happened to you today."

On the ride home that evening, Mark's stomach still hurt. While the rest of the family had enjoyed hot dogs and french fries, followed by ice-cream cones, Mark hadn't been able to enjoy any of the other good food. He wished now that he'd never bragged about how many pies he could eat. It seemed like every time he boasted about something, it ended badly.

Dear Lord, Mark silently prayed, *forgive me for bragging, and help me to remember to be humble, not full of pride.*

When they pulled into their yard sometime later, Dad halted the horse and buggy and pointed ahead.

"Look, Alice," he shouted, "your horse is running around the front yard, and she's trampled both yours and Mattie's pretty flowers."

"Ach, no," Mom gasped. "I wonder how she got out of her stall."

Mattie looked at Mark with tears in her eyes. "My little garden is ruined."

Mark gulped, remembering suddenly that the latch on the horse's stall was broken and he'd forgotten to tell Dad about it. Even though he'd tied the gate shut, apparently it hadn't held. In addition to his stomachache, he felt guilty about the gate, and now he'd need to tell Dad the truth.

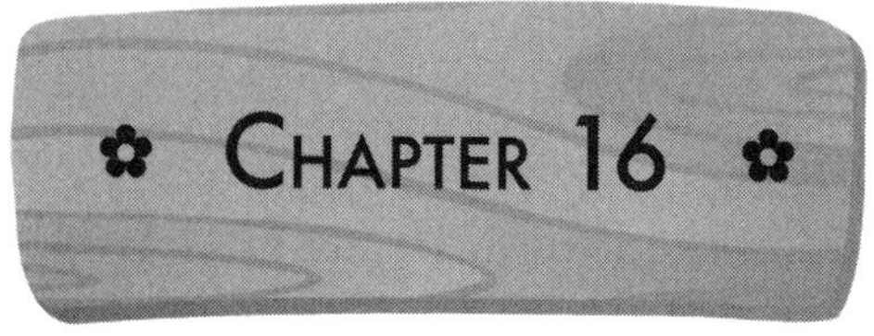

Chapter 16

Birthday Surprise

Mark could hardly believe their summer vacation had gone so fast, but he guessed that was because they'd all been so busy. He had helped Mom and Mattie plant new flowers in their gardens, since it was his fault the horse had gotten out and ruined the flowers. He even came up with some ideas about where to rotate some of the plants for something new in the vegetable garden.

Dad fixed the gate on the horse's stall, and Mark helped with that, too. Mark and Mattie had also done some work for Grandpa and Grandma Miller and earned money selling fruit, vegetables, and flowers from Mattie's garden at their produce stand. With the money he'd earned, Mark had been able to buy a larger basket for his bike, and Mattie had gotten another book about flowers.

The summer went way too quickly, and even though Dad had been too busy to take Mark and his brothers camping, at least they'd been able to do some fun things. Mark had been a little disappointed after hearing that John's grandpa had taken him camping. But it made

Mark all the more anxious for autumn, when Dad said he thought he'd have the time to take them.

Mark still had fun playing basketball with his brothers. He'd also gone fishing with John again, and searched for more rocks on his own. But he never bragged about any of those things. He'd learned his lesson after eating so much at the pie-eating contest.

Today, Mark and Mattie were going back to school, and even though it meant he wouldn't have as much free time anymore, Mark looked forward to the opportunity for more learning. He would make sure this year that he had the right spelling list in his hands for each week. He didn't want to take the wrong words home to study again. That had been terrible.

Their little brother, Perry, was starting school for the first time today, which would leave only Ada at home with Mom.

"Wanna go to school," Ada whined when Dad hitched his horse to the buggy to take Perry for the first time. Beginning tomorrow, Mom would either walk with him or he'd ride on the back of the twins' bicycle-built-for-two, with Mark riding up front. Later, when Perry was a little older, he might get a bike of his own.

"You still have a couple of years until you can go to school," Mom said, giving Ada a hug. "In the meantime, I'm going to enjoy having you home with me."

"Wish I didn't have to go back to school," Mattie complained, moving toward the back door. "I'd rather be home doing other things, like playing with Twinkles. I'll be glad when I graduate after completing the eighth grade."

"Please don't say things like that," Mom said, putting her fingers to her lips. "Perry is excited to be starting school, so you don't want to make him anxious."

Mattie looked through the open door, where Perry stood on the bottom porch step, watching Dad. "Sorry, Mom. I wasn't thinking about that. I don't think Perry heard me, though."

"I'm sure he didn't, but I wanted to remind you that it's important to encourage Perry and Ada, too, about going to school, instead of them hearing you complain about going. Your days of being home will come quicker than you realize," Mom said. "It seems that my *kinner* are growing too fast."

"Jah," Mark agreed, feeling happier yet. "Bet I've grown two or three inches this summer." He scooped up his lunch that Mom had packed, and Mattie did the same.

"You're not bragging, are you?" Mattie asked as they walked outside to join Dad and Perry.

He shook his head. "Nope. Just stating facts."

"Are you sure you two don't want a ride to school today?" Dad asked as Mark and Mattie took out their bikes. "Calvin has already headed out on his bicycle, but since I'm taking your little bruder to school, you two may as well ride along."

"Thanks anyway, Dad, but it's more fun to ride my bike," Mattie replied. "I can look at all the pretty flowers as I go to school, but I won't stop to pick any today."

"I prefer riding my bike, too," Mark agreed. "It gives me a chance to look for unusual rocks."

"Well, don't you two dawdle along the way," Dad said as he helped Perry into the buggy. "You don't want to be late on your first day back at school."

"We won't," Mattie called, climbing onto her bike.

As the twins pedaled out of the yard behind Dad's horse and buggy, Mark knew his little brother would get to school before them. But that was okay, because Dad wanted to talk to Anna Ruth about Perry for a bit and make sure that Perry knew what was expected of him on this first day of school.

"Just think," Mark called to Mattie, "we'll be turning ten next week. Sure hope Mom and Dad are gonna have a party for us."

"Oh, they are," Mattie replied. "I heard Mom telling Dad that both sets of our grandparents will be there to help us celebrate our birthday."

Mark grinned. He could hardly wait for that. Special occasions were always better when all their family could be there. Hearing the stories their grandparents told was enjoyable, too.

Their first week of school went well, and Perry seemed to like it, too. On the evening of Mark and Mattie's birthday, Mom baked potatoes in the oven, and Dad cooked hot dogs for the children and steaks for the adults on the barbecue grill. Grandma Troyer brought some of her homemade sauerkraut to go with the hot dogs, along with a tray of deviled eggs. Grandma Miller brought a tossed green salad, as well as pie for dessert, but Mattie had no idea what kind it was. There was a cover over the pie, and Grandma had put it in the refrigerator. Everything looked and smelled delicious. Mattie's mouth watered just thinking about eating all that food.

"While the weather is still warm," Mom said, "why don't we take our dishes and food outside to the picnic tables and eat there?"

"That sounds wonderful," Grandma Miller agreed. "Before you know it, the cold weather will be setting in."

"I'll take the picnic items outside," Mattie volunteered. "Ada, would you help me by carrying the mayonnaise?"

"Okay." Ada nodded and gave Mattie a sweet smile.

"That's fine," Mom said, smiling at Mattie and then handing Ada the mayonnaise. "While you're taking care of that, I'll set out the ketchup, mustard, and buns for the hot dogs. Your daed's got the barbecue going, and it shouldn't be long till the hot dogs and steaks are done."

Mattie started for the silverware drawer but stopped and gave each of her grandmothers a hug. "I'm so glad you could both be here tonight."

"I am, too," they said at the same time.

Mattie placed the silverware, paper plates, napkins, and plastic glasses in a basket and scooted out the door with Ada. When she stepped outside, she found Mark and both grandpas sitting on the front porch. Grandpa Troyer and Grandpa Miller were playing a game of checkers, while Mark looked on.

"I get to play the winner," he said, grinning at Mattie.

"I wish you all the best," Mattie said, stepping off the porch. She knew Mark was good at playing checkers, but their grandpas had many years of practice behind them. She figured Mark would have a hard time playing against whomever won.

Oh, boy, this is getting exciting, Mark thought as he watched Grandpa Troyer jump two of Grandpa Miller's checkers. The person who won this match would be hard to beat.

As the game continued, Grandpa Miller made a few good moves and ended up with three of Grandpa Troyer's checkers. On and on they played, until Grandpa Troyer had Grandpa Miller's few remaining checkers trapped.

"That's it. You won fair and square," Grandpa Miller announced when all his checkers were gone. He smiled at Grandpa Troyer and gave his shoulder a squeeze. "There's no doubt about it. You're a better checkers player than me."

"Nope," Grandpa Troyer responded. "I just made a few good moves tonight."

"There was more to it than that," Grandpa Miller said with a shake of his head. "You thought through each of your moves and outfoxed me good."

Mark couldn't help but notice the good-natured way both his grandfathers had been toward each other. Even though Grandpa Troyer had won, he'd shown no hochmut about it.

That's the way I want to be, Mark thought. *Not just when I grow up, but now, as a boy.* He was glad he'd finally come to realize that being humble, not prideful, was the way God wanted His people to be.

"Well, Son," Grandpa Troyer said, giving Mark's arm a light tap, "looks like it's your turn to play checkers with me."

Mark was about to say that he'd like to wait until after supper, when Dad hollered that the meat on the grill was done.

"We can play later or some other time," Grandpa Troyer said. "Sure don't want that meat to get cold, now do we?"

Mark shook his head. "I'm more than ready to eat."

"Everything is so good," Grandma Miller said as the family sat at the picnic tables enjoying their meal. "Mark and Mattie, this is a great way to spend your birthday, don't you think?"

The twins nodded in agreement. "We were born at a good time of year for picnics," Mark said.

"You're right, and the weather couldn't be more perfect. Being with our family makes me so happy," Grandma Troyer put in. She smiled at Grandpa Troyer and said, "Should we tell them our good news?"

He nodded and smiled. "We've found a buyer for our house in Burton, so within the next month or so, we'll be moving here to Walnut Creek."

Everyone clapped.

"Where will you live?" Russell asked, reaching for another hot dog.

Grandma Troyer smiled. "Your daed's going to add on to the house so that we'll have a place of our own."

"A *daadihaus*?" Mattie asked in surprise. She'd never expected that Grandma and Grandpa would be living in a grandparents' house right next to them. That really was good news, and the best birthday present she could ever receive.

"Jah," Mom spoke up. "It will be nice for me to have my parents living close by."

"For us, too," Grandpa Troyer said. "With my arthritis getting worse as I grow older, I can't do as many things as I did before. So living closer, where we'll have more help, will be a benefit for me and your *grossmudder*."

They talked about Grandpa and Grandma Troyer's

upcoming move throughout the meal.

After that, the family presented their gifts to the twins. The three older brothers gave Mattie some flower bulbs, seed packets, and garden gloves, while Mark got new fishing tackle and his very own basketball. Grandma and Grandpa Miller gave Mattie a cookbook and Mark a new straw hat and a pair of suspenders. Grandpa and Grandma Troyer presented Mattie with an apron and oven mitt with her name embroidered on it. Mark got a book about building things out of wood. Mom and Dad gave the twins the best gift of all—a pretty brown-and-white pony.

"Danki, Mom and Dad," Mark and Mattie said at the same time.

Mark gently stroked the pony's head. "Sure never expected that."

"Me neither." Mattie smiled. "What should we call the little fellow?" she asked, looking at Mark.

"How about 'Treasure,' because this pony is a real treasure?"

Mattie nodded enthusiastically. "I like that name!"

"And now," Grandma Miller said, "I think while you two put the pony in the barn, I'll go inside and get the pie I baked."

"I'll help you," Mom said, rising from her bench.

When the twins returned to the yard several minutes later, Grandma had placed her pie on the table and cut everyone a small piece. When she handed one to Mattie, and Mattie took a bite, a look of surprise came over her face.

Curious as to why, Mark dug into the pie he'd been given. It was blueberry—the very kind of pie he said he'd never be able to eat again. Not wanting to hurt Grandma's feelings, he forced himself to eat the piece he was given, and then he said, "Danki. I guess you wanted Mattie and me to be reminded of the humble pie we ate at the Mt. Hope auction."

"Oh, no," Grandma Miller said with a shake of her head. "I brought it because I thought everyone liked blueberry."

"It's not the only dessert, either," Mom put in. "In fact, I have a special birthday cake for you and Mattie right here." She removed the lid from the container she held, which Mark hadn't even noticed until now. Inside was a delicious-looking chocolate cake with ten candles in the center of it.

As everyone sang "Happy Birthday" to the twins, Mark looked over at Mattie and smiled. He wondered if she was thinking the same thing as him—that at least Grandma's pie was blueberry and not a real humble pie. The gifts they'd received, the cake, and most of all,

all the family being here, made this their best birthday ever. Mark couldn't wait to see what next year would bring.

Recipe for Mattie's German Raw Apple Cake

Ingredients
½ cup butter or margarine
½ cup brown sugar
1 cup granulated sugar
2¼ cups flour
¼ teaspoon salt
1 teaspoon cinnamon
2 teaspoons baking soda
1 cup sour milk (1 tablespoon vinegar mixed with enough milk to make 1 cup)
2 cups diced raw apples

Topping
½ cup granulated sugar
¼ cup packed brown sugar
½ teaspoon cinnamon

Preheat oven to 350 degrees. In mixing bowl, cream butter and sugars. In second bowl, combine flour, salt, and cinnamon. In a third bowl, add baking soda to sour milk.

Add dry ingredients (second bowl) and sour milk (third bowl) to creamed mixture (first bowl), and stir well. Fold in apples. Pour into greased 9x13-inch pan. Combine topping ingredients and sprinkle evenly on top. Place in oven and bake for 40 minutes.

About the Author

Wanda E. Brunstetter is an award-winning, bestselling author who enjoys writing historical, as well as Amish-themed novels. Descended from Anabaptists herself, Wanda became fascinated with the Plain People when she married her husband, Richard, who grew up in a Mennonite church in Pennsylvania. Wanda and her husband live in Washington State. They have two grown children, six grandchildren, and two great-grandchildren. Wanda and Richard often travel the country, visiting their many Amish friends and gathering further information about the Amish way of life. In her spare time, Wanda enjoys photography, ventriloquism, gardening, reading, and having fun with her family.

Visit Wanda's websites at www.wandabrunstetter.com and www.amishfictionforkids.com.